1

He sat his bay horse and studied Polonski's Swinging Bridge. The well-constructed rope-and-plank suspension structure swung across the rushing water of the Rio Grande River like a giant spider's web. When most folks thought about the Rio Grande, they had visions of the sluggish river that separated Texas from Mexico, not the foamy, surging force that over millions of years had cut a chasm to rival the Grand Canyon through the tablelands of northern New Mexico.

Why an immigrant from Poland had gone to such efforts to build the swinging bridge was beyond Slocum's imagination. No one seemed to know where the hermit had gone after completing the engineering feat. The structure, however, saved a hundred miles when crossing the river, especially when the stream churned with high water from rains and melting snow in the southern Rockies. Grateful for the bridge's construction, Slocum urged the bay onto the boards in the bridge's narrow confines and started for the eastern bank. For an instant, the horse beneath him hesitated, but Slocum spoke softly to him, nudged him with his spur, and the cow pony began the trek over the roaring waters. Slocum glanced off to the side and studied the angry river dancing beneath them. If anyone ever made a misstep and fell in, they would never survive the turbulence.

Out of habit, he looked back over his shoulder. Seeing nothing, he turned forward. He felt more of the give and the sway of the structure when they reached the center of the bridge. From there, he could survey the dark brown rock walls of the towering cliffs above them. The bay began to climb uphill with more sureness in his step than he had in the descent to the middle.

Gunshots cracked above the river's crescendo. The sound forced Slocum to reach for his Colt and twist around to see who was doing the shooting. Unable to tell, he urged the bay from the bridge. He had no intention of being caught in the open, if those shots were intended for him. At last, the pony's feet struck solid ground and he cat-hopped up the loose gravel to a high point, where Slocum reined him around.

Slocum could make out three men on horseback charging down the hillside trail for the bridge. In their wake, they'd scattered a poor man's string of burros laden with firewood. Slocum recalled passing the gray-haired old man earlier at the trailhead. The three riders' attitude upset him, but he had other concerns more pressing.

The lead horse of the three reared in protest at the prospect of entering the bridge, and the threesome piled up in a mass of cursing loud enough to be heard above the river's rush. Slocum holstered his Colt and started on. They were no business of his. Besides, they were probably liquored up and spoiling for trouble to judge from the way they acted. He set out up the trail along the face of the mountain, glancing back to see if the riders' furious attempts to get the sorrel horse on the bridge had worked. Despite their efforts, the red horse still wanted no part of the crossing. Served them right for stampeding the Mexican cutter's burros. A small smile creased Slocum's windburned face at their plight.

Soon the bay reached the canyon's rim, and Slocum allowed him to breathe. Standing up in the stirrups and even leaning forward, he could no longer see the bridge far below. Satisfied the horse was ready to go again, he headed across the sagebrush and brown grass of the tableland. If all went well, he would be at Marcia's house before the sun set over the San Juan Mountains far in the west.

He wondered who those three men were. Then he dismissed them. The past ten days on the move, circling around in the southern Rockies to lose two bounty chasers, had been serious business. The Abbott brothers were, he hoped, headed for Walsenburg. Meanwhile, he was far to the south, about to reach the Camino Real—the King's Highway to El Paso. Here the road was not much more than two ruts, but it eventually led to Mexico City, a highway of the conquistadors and used as a trade route for three centuries by the people in this land.

Along the upper route of the road, small villages clung to the icy creeks that rushed down from the Santo Cristo Mountains and fed the Rio Grande. Latinos and Pueblo Indians filled these small hubs of civilization. Benito was one of those places, and the one he sought. Marcia Onza lived there. Slocum rose in the stirrups in the light of afternoon and trotted his horse southward. To his left towered the Santo Cristo range, and far across the deep gorge and the wide tabletop rose the San Juans.

He dropped off the rise and headed downhill in a great sweeping route that would diminish the grade for wagons and animals. Below him, green cottonwoods lined the stream that gleamed like silver threading through the small verdant patches of alfalfa, beans, and corn. No sign of those rowdies since the bridge—he wondered if they were even headed this way.

At the base, he took the side road eastward. It wound past small adobe houses and homesteads on the watercourse. An occasional cur dog rushed out to bark at him. Noisy children quit playing, grew silent, and studied his passing with sharp coal eyes. He waved to them and made the bay trot.

At her driveway, he reined him down the sandy lane toward the high fencing that surrounded a yard set under some rustling cottonwoods. A cool south wind had swept his face since he left the bridge.

"Hello," he shouted above the two dogs barking behind the fencing.

"Hush! Hush!" she said in Spanish to the dogs, and rushed to met him with her skirt in her hand. A short woman, Marcia still possessed the figure of a girl in her teens.

She blinked her eyes in disbelief at the sight of him; then

a warm smile caused dimples in her olive cheeks. "Slocum! Slocum! Come in."

He dismounted and shook his legs to revive them. Then he looked down at her. The sight warmed him. Excitement danced in her dark eyes, and she threw up her arms and stood on her toes to kiss him. He bent over and took her in his arms. His mouth met hers and he hugged her small form to him.

"Where have you been?" she asked, out of breath.

"Coming to see you," he said, and led the bay inside the gate.

"So long you have been gone." She encircled his arm and hugged it hard to her as she led him to the corral.

"How are you?" he asked.

"Fine. Fat, but fine."

He stopped and held her out to look at her from head to toe. "It doesn't show."

"Good," she said, and looked at the ground. "But you are also a big liar."

"I will look closer later," he whispered in her ear.

She nodded, and mischief danced in her brown pupils. Quickly she took down the bars and allowed the bay inside the pen. Slocum stripped off the saddle and blankets, which he spread out on the top rail to dry.

"How long can you stay?" she asked.

"Who knows?" He reached for her, but she ducked out from under his arm. Then he watched her toss some sweet-smelling alfalfa hay to the bay. When finished, she clapped her hands to dust them off and turned to him.

"For a week?" she asked.

"What do you need done?"

"I would like a remada to cook and sleep under this summer when it is so hot."

"We would need to go up and cut some aspen poles," he said. He recalled all the work when he'd cleaned out her irrigation ditch with a long-handled shovel and repaired the banks. This time she only needed a crude brush arbor built for her summer purposes.

"I can borrow a team and wagon from my brother-in-law to go and get them," she said.

"Sure, why not."

"Wonderful. You spoil me. Come, I have some fresh tortillas and rice in the pot." She moved in, jammed her hip to his leg, and pulled him along by the arm.

"I thought you'd never feed me," he said.

"Oh, you haven't eaten in a long time?"

"Long enough, girl. Plenty long enough."

Her small adobe *casa* sat under the giant cottonwoods. She led him through the open door, and the pair of long-haired sheepdogs stopped. They acted anxious to be invited over the threshold, but she never paid them any heed. She went to work at stirring the kettle of rice hung over the small mesquite fire in the hearth. Then quickly, with deft fingers, she reheated a snowy flour tortilla on the grill. Motioning him toward the washbasin on the dry sink to clean up, she busied herself preparing him a plate of food.

"And how has it been going?" he asked, lathering his hands with her yucca soap.

"For a rich widow woman, fine."

"I always worry when I ride up here that some big hombre will meet me at that gate with a pistol. He will say, 'Go away. This is my *casa* and my Marcia.' "

"You worry about me?"

"I worry you have found a man." He bent over the basin and rinsed his stubbled face.

"Why do I need a man? If my gringo hombre will come by and see me and take care of my needs like build me a remada."

"Last time I cleaned out the irrigation ditch." He also recalled how each evening she had rubbed down the sore muscles in his back.

"And the time before that was lambing time," she said.

"Yes, and I think I will try to miss that. Where are your sheep?" he asked, drying his face on a coarse towel.

"Out to pasture with everyone else's. Boys herd them all summer."

"Good. I am looking forward to cutting some poles for your remada." He sure would not miss the stinking sheep.

"So am I," she said. She delivered the platter heaped with rice and chunks of brown meat, red and green chilies, and the snowy tortillas. It drew the saliva into his mouth and his empty stomach roiled. Rich food smells wafted up his nostrils and made him half sick with the thought of being full again. It had been too long.

"Which way did you ride in from?" she asked, pouring him coffee.

"North. Out of Colorado. Why?"

"There are some bad hombres around here." She rose and looked toward the doorway as if to make sure they were alone. "The main one is called Yarborough."

"What's he doing?" Slocum asked. Yarborough's name did not ring a bell nor draw up any memory of anyone with that moniker.

"He pistol-whipped a boy for nothing this week. I think he has raped some young girls in the valley, but their parents are both ashamed and afraid to tell the sheriff. Afraid that he will get them if they do."

"Three of them?"

"Yes, do you know them?"

"No, but earlier three men scattered a woodcutter's burros off the trail up at Polonski's Bridge. I was on this side, they were on the other. One of them rode a skittish sorrel and couldn't get him on the bridge."

"There is one called Dash and another called Mica. Mica rides the sorrel horse. Oh, he is a fancy one and has a silver-mounted bridle."

"What are they doing up here?"

"Forcing people to feed them and robbing them of their money."

"Why doesn't someone tell the sheriff?"

"They are afraid if Yarborough gets away from the law, he will come back and kill them." She shook her head ruefully and took a chair opposite him. "Sheriff Romerez is not a strong man. He is very honest, but he is not a gunfighter."

"The people should eliminate these coyotes."

"If my Lorenzo was here . . ."

Slocum's hand shot out and clasped her forearm on top of the table. Her husband Lorenzo had been a real man. He had ridden with Slocum as an army scout out of Fort Union against the Comanches.

The vivid image of fifty raging Comanche warriors swarming down on the two of them and the small company of soldiers filled his thoughts. Dust and the salt of sweat burned his eyes. He repeatedly emptied his Colt into their deadly thrusts. Lorenzo knelt beside him doing the same. They would reload and then fight off another wave. The wounded and moaning soldiers were all around them; Slocum had figured it would be his last day on earth, and he'd been prepared for Hell itself as a respite from the heated battle.

Men begged for water, the sun bore down on them. The Comanches prepared at a distance for another charge. Their war cries sounded like so many coyotes squalling. They milled about on the flat prairie discussing what they would do next. Slocum figured they were building up their courage. A scorching-hot wind swept the gun smoke away and helped clear Slocum's vision. In the lull, he stepped over and jerked a .44/.40 out from beneath a pinned-down horse.

"Give that to me," Lorenzo said, and took the Winchester.

"They're coming back," Slocum shouted, unsure where the lieutenant or Sergeant Clawson were or what condition they were in. "Hold your fire until they're close. We ain't got bullets to waste."

"They are going to charge right through us," Lorenzo said, sighting down the barrel. "I will get that chief this time."

Slocum nodded. "Everyone hold your fire until they get close enough," he repeated. His nostrils were scorched from the spent gun smoke and his throat was dry and raw. These could be his last minutes on earth.

The remaining troopers were steady enough, but with only sixty rounds of ammo issued per man, they would soon have to throw horse turds at the Comanches. Damn the army anyway, sending men out without enough ammunition for a fight like this. They'd spent months on the high plains going in and out of Fort Union and not finding a thing. This was the first major fight, and obviously the Comanches were set to repel the soldiers at any price. Bodies of bucks and dead horses littered the prairie beyond the bodies that the scouts and troopers used for fortifications.

Blood-curdling screams shattered the air. Then the drum of hooves as Slocum reminded the troopers again and again, "Hold your fire." Facing a line of war-painted Comanches screaming until the cold chills ran up his spine and threatened his sanity was hell enough for any human. The warriors drew closer until he could see the black anger on their painted faces.

"Fire!" he screamed, and his right hand became an exploding extension of his arm. One buck went down, but the others pressed on in a suicidal strike. The chief wore a buffalo-horn headdress, and he came at them to the left. Slocum watched Lorenzo raise up, take aim, and begin to fire the Winchester. His bullet took the chief in the face, and the chief's horse shied away into another. Then the crest of rampaging horses and Comanches drove Slocum aside and he was knocked silly for a long second. Fighting to his feet, he could see the lance protruding from Lorenzo's chest. The feathers on the shaft fluttered in the wind. Slocum shot the attacker in the back once, twice, three times, and his revolver clicked on empty. A soldier rose up, swarmed over the fallen Comanche, and beat his head to a pulp with a pistol butt.

Then there was only the rush of the wind. No more war cries. Slocum fumbled to reload the Colt. He dropped cartridges—it didn't matter. He fell to his knees beside his friend. Life waned in Lorenzo's eyes. Absently Slocum holstered the pistol and then gently removed the lance. Blood began to spill out of Lorenzo's vest. Slocum tossed it aside, sick with the knowledge of the damage the long blade had wrought inside the man.

"Hold still, friend." Slocum bent over to comfort him.

"Marcia—mia Marcia." His right hand squeezed Slocum's left, and then he let go. Lorenzo was gone. Jaws clenched, Slocum rose and looked about. Of the thirty troopers, less than ten were still standing.

"Do we have a horse alive?" he demanded.

"Slocum, we have one," a young private said, and pulled a horse up to its feet.

"Any more?"

"Maybe one or two more. They've all been shot some."

"Private, cinch that horse up and ride like hell for help."

"Yes, sir."

"Wait. How much ammo do you have?"

"Three cartridges."

"You men find him a couple more loaded pistols in case he meets more of them red bastards," Slocum shouted.

They rushed about to obey his command. He found the lieutenant from Vermont, a smooth-faced boy—dead. The West Pointer would never need his revolver again. Slocum also emptied his cartridge pouch. Then he hurried across the field of dead and wounded to the private, and handed him the Colt, which made the third one in his belt.

"They all loaded?" he asked the youth.

"Yes."

"Don't spare that horse. Get back to Fort Union and send medical help."

"I will," the boy said, and lashed the horse away.

Slocum stood and studied the disappearing figure, puffs of dust swept away after him. He only hoped the horse lasted to Fort Union. Then he turned back to the grisly task at hand of tending to the wounded and dying.

The official report showed killed in action against the Comanche war party; Lieutenant James Morris, Landers, Vermont: Sergeant Dane Clawson, Whistler, Ohio; Corporals Kimes, O'Grady, Holmes, and Dawinski; Privates Mario, Donovan, O'Grady, Laughton, McQuire, and Hillski. And Scout Lorenzo Onza.

Troopers tended the wounded as best they could under field conditions. Satisfied they had done all they could for them, Slocum walked out into the battlefield. He found a stock saddle on a dead Comanche war horse. Squatting down on his haunches and rummaging in the saddlebags, he discovered a pouch of gold coins.

Quickly he searched around. None of the others were close by or paying any attention to him. Good. He loosened the strings that tied the saddlebags to the back of the saddle, and then used his knife to cut them on the other side. In a short while, he had worked the bags out from under the horse. They were heavy enough when he shouldered them that without looking inside, he knew they represented lots of money. Obviously, whoever the Comanche had stolen it from had been packing a fortune. Slocum didn't want the soldiers suspicious, so he went about looking at the other dead warriors and gathering up usable firearms.

The men built buffalo chip fires to boil coffee. Slocum and a private cut some steaks off the fattest dead horse to roast over the coals. They had four serviceable horses left. His own horse and Lorenzo's dun were dead. The severely wounded horses had been destroyed. One of the soldiers rode out and captured a Comanche's big gray that obviously was a Texas ranch horse from his brand, and gave him to Slocum to ride.

Slocum put his saddle and pads on the big gelding, then tied on the saddlebags as casually as he could. He gathered the Winchester rifle and the private things of Lorenzo to take back to his widow Marcia. About dark, he could hear the rumble of ambulances and mules coming. Didn't take them long to get out there, he decided. Prairie wolves howled and yipped at the moon as the two companies of soldiers arrived.

"They wanted blood today," Captain Jergenson said, moving about the camp with Slocum. The two doctors with them tended to the wounded.

"Yes, they did, Captain."

"You did good here, Slocum. Lucky anyone is alive." Jergenson shook his head.

"No, I didn't do anything right. Never had any idea they would stand and fight."

"They haven't in the past." The captain looked hard at the lieutenant's dead horse under the light of the orderly's lamp. "Shame, that was a good animal. I remember when he got that one."

"Why were you so close to us?"

"New orders," the captain explained "Colonel Mackenzie has everyone in the field. We are going to come at them from all directions and shatter the hostiles' resistance. Our orders are to be in the field for three weeks."

"Give me time off to take Lorenzo's things to his widow?" Slocum asked the officer. "I'll be back and join you."

"You'll have to ride fast."

"Captain, I have a good mount taken from the Indians. I could leave when the moon gets up and be to her place in two days."

"Slocum?"

"Yes, sir?"

"You will come back and help me?"

"I will, sir."

"Good. Go take her those things. Godspeed, and tell her how brave he was."

"I will, Captain." They shook hands.

When he rode out that night, Slocum recalled reaching back and feeling for the bags. He could hear the ring of the gold when he loped the gray. In less than two days he was at her gate, and she knew at the sight of him without her man what he had come to tell her.

The gold was their secret, and she bought more sheep and cattle to put in the community herd with *her husband's last pay*. The rest she hid and spent judiciously enough not to bring on suspicion. A woman of many sheep and cattle—she was rich enough and would probably never use all the twenty-dollar gold pieces he'd found on the Comanche's stolen saddle.

"Two men in my life," Marcia said now, bringing him back from his memories of the past. "Lorenzo, who I have lost, and you, hombre, who I cannot keep."

"If I had a shave and bath . . ." Finished eating, he shoved the plate away and stretched his arms over his head. His stomach felt comfortably full.

She made a face at him. "Then you would want to share my bed?"

"I'd sure hate to have to sleep with those dogs."

"No, I would feel sorry for them." She bounded up and went for her cast-iron kettle to fill the basin. Soon, hot water steamed up in the tin basin, and she set out her shaving kit to work on him.

"One shave—and perhaps a haircut too, hombre." She tilted her head to the side to look at him. "And a bath for you. You smell like a horse."

Hours later, she lay inside his arms. Her warm naked form curled up against him under the thick woven cotton blanket that protected against the night's cool air. He listened to the gentle wind rustling the cottonwoods in the yard. At some distance, he could hear dogs barking. Hers growled outside the doorway, then settled down. At last sleep came to him.

2

A small adobe chapel, the bell tower topped with a cross and adorned by a half-dozen purple pigeons, highlighted the square. Two stores, three cantinas, a blacksmith shop, and the community wool warehouse made up Benito, with a large open lot to park wagons on Saturday. That was the day most valley residents came to town for supplies, and they came back again on Sunday for Mass. At mid-week this all stood deserted.

Before the building marked Stone and Goldstein's, Slocum reined up the buggy horse and tied off the reins. The light spring wagon was Marcia's mark of wealth. Others drove lumbering, rickety farm wagons, and a few owned buckboards, but the like-new single-seat spring wagon was a small sign of her affluence.

"You go get a drink in the cantina," she said to him, with a hand on his knee. "I will purchase the things we will need for the trip."

"Fine, Mrs. Onza."

They shared a private smile. He watched her disappear in the front door of S. and G.'s. Satisfied nothing was out of place, he ambled across the empty street for the Silver Moon Cantina and parted the doors. Inside the shadowy interior, he let his eyes grow accustomed to the room's darkness. A stale smell of burned-out cigar butts and the sourness of beer filled his nose.

"What will it be, amigo?" the waxed-mustached bartender asked.

"A beer perhaps. No, give me some good rye."

"I have rye."

"Is it good?"

"I have rye." He reached behind him and drew out the bottle for Slocum to look at the label.

Slocum didn't recognize the brand, but he nodded anyhow. A good drink might settle him down. He still felt as if he was being chased by bounty men. The past ten days coming out of Colorado had been a purposeful dodging journey to lose the pair on his heels, the Abbott brothers out of Fort Scott, Kansas.

He paid the bartender for the drink. His finances were low, but a good card game or two and he would have change to jingle again. Down at Santa Fe, he planned to stop over and play some poker. It was a lively town for gambling. But first, Marcia needed a remada built, and his horse could stand some rest. Before he rode out, he planned to shoe him too.

Some men rode up outside. Talking loudly among themselves, they came inside the bar. A large burly man with a black mustache parted the doors, eyed Slocum hard, and walked to the bar. His two companions followed him like cocky banty roosters trailing the main one.

"Whiskey, Tomas," the man said, and the other two stopped talking when they saw Slocum at the bar. In the mirror, he read their dour reaction to his presence.

"*Sí,* Señor Yarborough," the bartender said.

So the big man had arrived. Slocum considered them in the mirror. Every muscle in his body tingled. Bullies seldom picked on well-armed men, but at three to one, they outnumbered him enough to give them courage if they wanted it.

"You're new here," Yarborough said.

"Passing through," Slocum replied.

"I never seen your horse outside." Yarborough gave a head toss toward the door.

"He must have wandered off," Slocum said.

"Yeah. You planning on staying around here long?"

"You the law?" The man's ways were needling him.

Yarborough laughed openly, and the other two on the far side of him joined in. The bartender's eyes darted back and forth. Obviously he was concerned that some sort of fracas might erupt in his bar.

"No, I ain't the law," Yarborough said. "Just like to know who's around."

"I'll be around," Slocum said. He set the glass down, nodded thanks to the barkeep, then started for the door.

He laid his hand on the bat-wing door. The skin on the back of his neck crawled when Yarborough spoke out again.

"I never caught your name, mister."

"Slocum," he said, and turned to look at the threesome.

"Guess we never met before, Slo-cum."

Slocum shook his head and held his tongue. The urge to tell the man he didn't linger in the sewers much either came and went.

"Yarborough's mine."

Slocum nodded. His left hand still on the bat-wing door, he wondered for a long moment if the man had more to say.

"See you, Slocum."

"Yes, you may," Slocum said, and headed for the wagon. He strode across the hard-packed street and considered that the threesome might try to bother Marcia. If they ever did, he would kill them. Also, he knew that the people of Benito would soon tire of these bullies if what she'd said was true. Yarborough probably knew how long he had in this place before the meek took charge. Oppression brought out resistance, like a thorn that festered in a man's leg until it erupted like a volcano.

A young flush-faced boy carried out Marcia's purchases and loaded them in the back of the wagon. She adjusted the shawl over her shoulders as she came out of the store's front door. She was a small but pretty woman. Though there was nothing small about the fire she aroused in him. With a hand, he helped her in the wagon, knowing that Yarborough was watching it all from behind the bat-wing doors of the Silver Moon. Slocum considered his peering obscene, and the notion drew up some of his anger.

"You will have to watch," he said under his breath. On the

seat, he reined the buggy horse around and started to leave.

"What for?"

"Yarborough knows you exist now."

"He was in the cantina?" she asked.

"He came in, introduced himself. But now he knows or will know about the Widow Onza."

"What would he want with a poor widow woman?"

"Hard to tell. Keep a loaded gun handy."

"I always do."

"Good." Still, he felt queasy about the man's presence in the village. Yarborough and his men were up to no good any time they could find it.

After lunch, Slocum reshod his horse. With the shoes set and the hooves trimmed, he straightened his tired back, admired his handiwork, and smiled at Marcia. She sat on a nearby box with her legs gathered up in her arms and rocked on her butt.

"What will you do next?" She put her feet down and hopped off the container to join him.

"Better go over my guns and clean them," he said. When a man lived by his wits on the go, clean, well-oiled firearms were a necessity of life. Like shoeing the horse, it made up an essential a part of his existence that he could not afford to neglect.

"Here, let me carry that rifle," she said when he drew it out of the scabbard on the corral fence.

"It's heavy."

"I know," she said, and cradled the long gun in her arms. "I will make some hot water."

"Good, I'll need it boiling to purge out these barrels."

The dogs began to bark at the approach of a wagon. She nodded to Slocum that it was all right.

"It is only my brother-in-law coming to trade me rigs so we have a big wagon to take to the mountains."

"Good," he said, and drew in a deep breath. He would not soon forget Yarborough and his two hardcases.

Slocum and Marcia left for the mountains in the early morning. The two dogs, excited to be out of the yard, bounded along beside the wagon. He drove, and she sat beside him on the high seat as they pulled out on the main road. Her brother-in-law's team of duns acted well-broke and powerful for small horses.

She scolded the dogs not to pick fights with the curs that ran out to challenge them. A few stiff-haired moments, and then hers returned to the wagon's perimeter.

They crossed a sandy dry wash, and then harness jingled as the duns trotted up the road. Scolded by a mockingbird or two from the trees, some ravens patrolled the road looking for a meal.

"I am so lucky today," she said. "I have a good man with me and we are on our way to the mountains to get the material to build my new remada."

He raised his gaze to the towering mountains, some still capped with snow. There would be a fun-filled few days ahead of them.

"I don't think your bother-in-law approved of me," he said.

"Oh, Miguel, he is always worried that someone will come along and marry me." She hugged his arm and rocked with the sway of the rig. "Then when he needs to borrow some money, my husband won't let him have it."

"Does he borrow money often?"

"No, but sometimes when things are very tight, he will come. He never even tells my sister Consuela. But when he sells his wool or some sheep, he comes right over and repays me. He is a good man and cares for my sister very well."

"He must look out for you too."

"Oh, yes, he would have brought his boys and built my remada. But I was waiting for you."

"You might have waited a long time." He flipped the reins at the horses as they started slowing down.

"No, I burned a candle at the church only a few weeks ago for you to return and see me."

"For me to come by?"

"Yes." She hugged him tightly in her arms.

"But isn't that—I mean, does the church approve of such things?"

"What Father Merino knows and doesn't know is not so

important. I wanted you to come see me again."

"Oh, all right." He drew the ponies down for the steep hill ahead.

"We can camp on the stream up there." She indicated the mountains ahead.

"Good. You have any fishhooks?"

"Of course."

He settled back in the seat and drove the team. With a lovely woman to share his day, the prospect of some calmer times ahead suited him well. With no sign of the Abbott brothers, he would enjoy the reprieve.

At midday they reached the camp beside the gurgling stream. He set up the canvas shelter between two pines with a rope, then pegged down the corners and drew them tight. She hurried about unloading food, bedding, and cooking gear. He unharnessed the two horses and hobbled them. That completed, he took a moment to wipe his brow on his sleeve and study the towering canyon clad with pines and clusters of snowy-barked aspens in the depressions.

He hung the harness on the wagon and turned to watch her undressing at the stream. She shed the blouse. In the glaring sunshine, her small breasts looked pointed, and shook as she worked down the long brown skirt from her hips and legs. Soon she stood naked in the sparkling light, then ventured into the rushing water. Past knee-deep in the force of the stream, she scooped up handfuls of water, and the drops shone like diamonds on her olive skin.

She washed her face and then her arms. Her rock-hard nipples grew sharper when she stood up and smiled at him. The rush of the stream filled his ears. He handed her a towel as she emerged, and she began to dry herself. When he could no longer stand by and gaze at her nudity, he swept her up in his arms and carried her to the shelter.

He shifted her in his arms while he toed off his boots, then knelt down and placed her gently on top of the blankets spread on the ground. His breath rushed through his nose as he considered her ripe body while he stood up above her, unbuckled his gunbelt in great haste, and shed his pants, vest, and shirt.

Then he knelt between her knees. His thoughts of the pleasures ahead filled him full of drive. She spread her legs apart for him with a knowing smile, then reached up and pulled him down on top of her. Their mouths met and tongues clashed like swords. With her cool skin pressed to him, his hips ached to hunch it to her. His throbbing manhood soon found her gates, and his entry drew a sigh from her parted lips. He began to work himself deeper, savoring the constricting walls and her efforts to arch her back to rise up and meet him.

They pitched headlong into a spiraling whirlpool of greater-than-ordinary pleasure. He grasped both sides of her rock-hard butt to drive deeper and deeper into her boiling volcano. His eyes squeezed shut to the tantalizing pleasure as he felt the head of his dick swell larger than ever before, and her breathing grew ragged in response. Then she went limp under him, and he was forced to draw in more air to salve his pained lungs.

Like a slow-consuming fire, her bleary eyes began to clear, and her hips again rose and fell to his efforts. She arched her back again, and their pubic bones ground together when he plunged to the very bottom of her well. Then, like a sparkling dynamite fuse being consumed by fire, a red-hot poker rose from inside his scrotum, flew out the end of his skintight dick, and exploded inside her.

"We ain't getting many poles cut this way," he mumbled later, sprawled on his back beside her.

She climbed on top of him, her small hand exploring his manhood. "We have much time." With insistence, she began to pull it back to life. Satisfied with its newfound stiffness, she straightened, moved forward, then eased herself down on it. With his erection inside her, she fed him her right breast to taste. Her eyes closed in deep pleasure at the efforts of his mouth and tongue on her nipple. She began to raise her hips up and down on top of him. Then she leaned over and whispered, "This is really what I have prayed for."

3

The ax in his grasp, he swung, and the bit drove great chips of aspen flying away. He paused to wipe his forehead on his sleeve. It was cool enough up there in the mountains, but the work of a lumberjack drew out the sweat from his leisurely spent days of gambling and dealing cards.

It had been going great until the Abbott brothers had shown up in Fort Collins. He had wandered down the face of the Rockies thinking he would lose them. But he'd finally decided to make some false trails westward, to lure the pair over the top, and meanwhile he'd dropped southward into New Mexico as secretly as possible. They weren't too likely to look for him in Benito, if they *did* discover his direction of travel, since it was off the Camino Real. And certainly they would never look up in this canyon.

His next blow downed the tree and he began whacking off the branches. Soon it was denuded of limbs, and he shouldered the two limber posts he had cut down. With the ax in his hand and balancing the long poles, he headed off the mountainside.

He crossed the stream on a fallen log, and dumped the poles on the rig he had built for her to use while stripping away the bark with a draw knife. She looked up and smiled. The ground around them was littered with long strips of the white aspen skin.

"I am afraid soon we will have enough and have to go home." She put down her tool, rushed over, and hugged him.

He rocked her back and forth in his arms while he studied the timber and the bare yellow slopes exposed above them. It would be a shame to have to leave this idyllic place, where their spontaneous lovemaking broke up the drudgery of the pole-gathering.

"Be a big shame too," he said. "But we better go home tomorrow."

"Oh," she said in disappointment.

"This afternoon I'll catch some fish."

"Good."

After some fire-roasted deer haunch, they dug for earthworms in the marshy ground below their camp. Soon, armed with a dozen worms in a tin can, they slipped along the bank to above where a large tree lodged in the water was causing a major eddy. Slocum undid the line wrapped around the willow pole and strung a fat worm on the hook. Then he swung the pole and sent the hook tumbling downstream toward the circling swirl.

A silver streak rose up and inhaled it. The trout went end over end dancing on top of the water. Slocum's pole bent double in an effort to turn the fish. Excited, Marcia shouted how large it was.

After the trout rushed up and down the creek several times, it finally gave up, and Slocum guided it onto the beach. At close to eighteen inches in length, it was a large fish for this small stream.

"I will clean it. Catch another and we will have a real feast," Marcia said, taking it by the gills and undoing the hook from its jaw.

"I'll try," he said.

The hook was rebaited and sent downstream, and went around the log unattached. Slocum recovered it and sent it down again. But the worm floated by without drawing a fish. He recovered it, split a 30-caliber bullet with his knife, then clasped it onto his catgut line about a foot and half above his hook. He added some more line, then send it downstream again for the eddy.

The first tug was halfhearted, but the second one was a nononsense solid strike and he set the hook. This time the fish ran harder and faster, and with more line had more freedom. Slocum moved back up the bank and the fish cleared the water, danced on his tail, and sent a spray of droplets each of which had little rainbows.

Marcia began shouting about the size of this one. Slocum was more concerned about the limber pole taming it enough to land it. Then the strong-jawed fish began to weaken, and soon was flopping on the beach. She pounced on it and quickly held up his prize.

"It is bigger yet," she bragged. "How did you learn how to fish?"

"Another way to survive."

"Good. We will have lots of fish to eat tonight."

He enjoyed catching trout—especially if she cooked them for him. He put up the fishing gear and went to stripping bark off the next pole while she cleaned his catch.

Busy at his task, he looked up at the dogs' barking, and spotted a rider coming up the dim road from below. Out of habit, he undid the thong on his Colt, so it would be ready in case he needed it.

"What is wrong?" she asked, on her knees with fish entrails in her hand.

"Someone's coming." He watched her stand up for a better look.

"Oh. I see him. It is one of my nephews. Hush, dogs." She laid the dressed fish out, washed her hands, and then hurried off to greet the boy. The youth of perhaps eighteen looked upset when he dismounted.

"What is wrong, Juan?" she asked, with Slocum on her heels.

"Yarborough and his men have kidnaped some of the girls. They are demanding tribute for them."

"How much are they asking for?" Slocum asked.

"A thousand dollars."

"No one has that much money, even in Santa Fe, let alone up here," Marcia said. She shook her head in disbelief that anyone would even ask for so much.

"Who are they holding?" Slocum asked.

"Señor Goldstein's daughter, for one."

Marcia looked shocked. "Oh, no, not the lovely girl—"

Juan nodded with a grim look.

"Juan's girlfriend," she informed Slocum.

"They won't have her long," Slocum said with a scowl. "Let's fix those fish now. We'll go in after dark and settle this matter."

"*Gracias, Señor.* I knew you would help us." The boy's face beamed.

"Juan, stay and eat with us," she said.

"Oh—"

"Stay," Slocum said to the youth. "You can help us load and lead the way in the dark. I kind of want to surprise them."

"*Gracias, Señor.* I told my father that my late uncle's best friend would stop these men."

"Well, I'm going to try, Juan."

"What can I do to help you, Señor?"

"Help me take down the shelter while she cooks those fish. No sense going to war on an empty belly." Slocum wondered what the rescue would entail. No telling—three worthless bullies would be apt to do anything.

The wagon was loaded with their things on top of the poles. Then Slocum and the boy captured the horses and harnessed them in preparation for the drive back.

"Has Yarborough posted any guards?" Slocum asked.

"His men were moving around a lot."

"Good. Then we better watch out for them when we get close to town. I would like to surprise him and have the upper hand."

"Yes."

She called for them to come and eat. The fish were crisp brown, served with her chilies, beans, and tortillas. When his belly was full, Slocum considered the low sun. They would need to stop short of the village even in the dark to observe the outlaws' actions.

"When we get close to town tonight, can you go in and get some others to help us?" Slocum asked Juan.

"Some, but they are not fighting men like you, Señor."

"They don't have to be. Numbers will count. Have them

bring anything, a muzzle-loader, a shotgun, a .22, or even an ax."

Juan nodded his head. "There are many of the people upset by these bad men."

"Fine. Tell them I will lead the way."

"They will come."

"Good. But first we must know where those three are at. We need all of them in the . . ." Slocum trailed off. He needed their headquarters surrounded and to be holding some kind of high card to take the outlaws on.

"They are in the Silver Moon Cantina, Señor."

"Good. That place can be breached if we need to."

"But what if they hurt the girls?"

"No, we aren't letting that happen. I have a plan," Slocum said, and shared a nod with Marcia. He didn't have a plan, but there was no sense in telling the boy that and worrying him. He would pretend to have everything worked out, and let the situation develop.

Close to midnight, they stopped off the road short of the town, unhitched the team from the wagon, and tied the horses to a tree. Slocum sent Juan on a path along the creek that few used. His job was to gather supporters and rejoin Slocum with them at the plaza.

"Stay here," Slocum said to Marcia, but he knew she wouldn't.

"No. If there is one of them on guard, he won't shoot a woman. Not a pretty woman."

"Too much risk."

"No risk. I will do it. You follow me. It will be much quicker."

Before he could protest, she started ahead, making the dogs stay back with him. He followed her, seeing her occasional silhouette in the moonlight that shone in pools of white on the road. The two dogs were delegated to walk with him. They growled at curs that challenged them, but kept their pace. Slocum stayed in the shadows close enough on her heels, but offering no target.

The dogs issued a throaty growl and he hushed them, dropping to his knees to better see and control the pair. If she were approaching a sentinel, he wished he could warn her. Then he saw someone step out from the darkness, and he knew from his outline it was one of Yarborough's men. The man spoke softly enough that Slocum could not hear the conversation, but he knew the outlaw was taking her back into shadows with him. Slocum ran his teeth over his lower lip. What should he do next? He wanted no harm to come to her.

He made the dogs sit and stay. They acted unhappy, but at last lay down, anxious for another command. He eased along the head-high adobe wall, crouched low, and moved closer until he could hear the man talking to her. Slocum squatted on his heels, waited, and watched the outlaw set his rifle down against the side of the adobe hovel.

"You ain't bad-looking."

The man's words to her made Slocum see red. He eased along, careful not to shuffle his feet. The Colt's wooden grips were tight in his fist.

"You aren't so bad-looking yourself, hombre. I bet you are a real stallion," she said.

"Yeah, I'm a real stallion. Yeah, I like you, gal. Let me see your titties."

Slocum made his move as she started to raise the hem of her blouse. His gun barrel hit the top of the man's head, and he went down like a poled steer. Good enough for the bastard too.

"You took a long time to get here," she said, sounding shaken. "How many more guards does he have out?"

"There are only three of them. This makes two left."

"What now?" she asked.

The man moaned. Slocum disarmed him and dragged him up to his knees. "Mister, your life ain't worth a blade of grass in a big fire. So you better listen close to me."

"What?"

"You try anything, you're dead." Slocum jerked him up by the collar.

"I understand. What're you going to do?"

"I aim to trade you to Yarborough, along with a chance to escape, providing those girls aren't hurt."

"Hurt?"

"Raped or harmed in any way."

"They ain't hurt, I swear, mister. They ain't been touched."

"They better not be. Where's the other gang members at?"

"Mica—he's in the cantina with Yarborough."

"You think he's lying about the girls?" she asked Slocum.

"No, no, I ain't lying," the man protested. "We wanted the money was all so we could ride on."

"Shut up," Slocum said, and shoved him ahead.

"What should I do?" she asked.

"Get your dogs. I left then back there and told them to stay. They mind well."

She gave a shrill whistle, and her dogs came on the run. "See, you did not get rid of me. And you won't. Give me his pistol. I want to shoot him if he tries to run."

They reached the square, and Slocum forced the prisoner, Dash, to sit on his butt out in the moonlit street. The lights were out in the cantina. In a few minutes, Slocum could hear the soft footfalls of many people coming to the plaza. Juan had brought even more than Slocum had expected. They moved in the shadows and took up defensive positions. Slocum directed Marcia to get behind a barrel.

Out of breath, Juan joined him. "Who's this?" Joan asked, motioning toward the outlaw.

"Dash. He was walking around guarding things."

"What will we do with them all?" the boy whispered.

"I say we trade them their freedom for the girls unharmed. Will your men agree to that?"

"Oh, yes. I am sure they want the girls back for their families, and they are not fighters, Señor."

"Tell them not to shoot. Spread the word. No one is to shoot unless I say so. I am going to get Yarborough's attention."

Juan whispered in Spanish that they all should hold their fire, and word quickly spread through the crowd. They had enough of a show of force to handle the outlaws, Slocum felt certain. It was time to start his plan. He hoped it worked.

"Go to screaming for Yarborough real loud, Dash," Slocum ordered.

"He might shoot me."

"If you don't, I'll shoot you." Slocum clicked the hammer back on his Colt to emphasize his point.

"Yarborough! Yarborough!"

"What the hell you doing out there, Dash?"

"He's my prisoner," Slocum called out. "And I have thirty-forty guns out here, ready to gun you down—tell him I'm not lying, Dash."

"It's the truth, Yarborough."

"Okay, Slo-cum, what's the deal."

"You and that other ranny in there throw out your guns and come out with your hands high."

"No deal. I've got four girls in here worth a thousand dollars. You want to see them—"

"Yarborough, you aren't making the deals. Those girls have one nick on them, these men are cutting your balls off with a dull knife. Listen to me. Hand those girls over, you come out here unarmed, and you ride off scot-free. After daylight, the sheriff will be here. Then you can deal with the law."

"You want to see these girls—"

"Yarborough. If you don't want to piss out of a tube, you better listen to me. I ain't cutting you any better deal than that one."

"Listen, Slocum—I'll shoot your gawdamn ass off."

"You have five minutes and we start whittling on Dash here."

"Yarborough! He ain't faking. They got more men with guns coming all the time."

"How do I know we can ride off?"

"Listen, send those girls out here and then we'll decide if you ride off." Slocum had heard the change in the outlaw's tone of voice—he was measuring his rope. Someone as shifty as Yarborough had not survived this long by being stupid when the chips were down.

"Send those girls out first," Slocum called. "If they haven't been harmed, you can ride out."

"I'll send all but one out. I'm keeping her for my hole card."

"Juan," Slocum said under his breath. "Go get their horses. Bring them up here."

"What if he keeps the last one?" Marcia hissed at him.

"He won't live to leave here if he does."

"But—"

"Yarborough, send them out, but don't you hurt that last one." Slocum turned to Marcia. "He's sending them out. You get them out of the way and I need to know if they were hurt in any way."

She rushed out in the street and clutched the first girl by the hand. The other two ran after them, and he could hear them sobbing in relief beside the building.

"Where's them horses?" Yarborough shouted back.

"They're coming. You try to take that last girl with you, Yarborough, and we're cutting you down in the street."

"Deliver those horses. That's the deal."

"They're coming."

In the moonlight, Juan brought two and quickly hitched them to the rack. A second man tied up the third one.

"They are all right," Marcia reported to Slocum.

"The last girl?" Slocum asked her over his shoulder.

"They say she is fine too."

"You're lucky, Yarborough. Toss those guns out and come out slow."

"Slocum—if I ever catch you—" Slocum heard the sound of two guns hitting the ground. The outlaws weren't unarmed, but Slocum knew that was the risk he had to take in this darkness.

"Save your breath and let that girl go!"

"I'll do it outside of town."

"No." He jerked Dash to his feet and used him for a shield, forcing the outlaw ahead. He stopped a few feet from the horses. Both Mica and the big man were now standing on the boardwalk, ready to untie their horses.

"Let her go now! Or the deal's off."

"Here's the skinny little bitch." The outlaw shoved her at him. Slocum gave Dash a swift boot in the butt and drove him toward Yarborough. Then he grasped the shaking girl by the forearm and swung her behind him. With his other hand, he banished the Colt at the three outlaws. They wasted no time, mounting up and charging out of the plaza.

Slocum realized how hard he gripped the girl's arm, and

released her. He listened for the fading sound of horses, then holstered his revolver. In his mind he knew he had not seen the last of Yarborough and his crew, and one day he might even regret letting them go, but all of the girls were safe.

A cheer went up, and everyone rushed from cover. Juan hugged the shaking girl beside him, and the youth began to pat her hair and talk softly to her.

"Señor, how much do I owe you? My daughter is safe. Oh, heavens, what can I do to repay you?" the merchant Goldstein asked Slocum.

"Be nice to Juan. He was the one who really saved her."

"Oh, yes, I will."

Slocum backed away from the crowd. The matter was over; he felt the strength drain from his body. Marcia hooked her arm in his and led him into the shadows. He bent over and kissed her on the mouth.

"You were sweet to tell that man about Juan."

"He deserved it."

"I know, but it was still sweet."

"Let's go home and go to bed. I am tired."

"And even sleep later?" she teased.

"Yes, even sleep later."

4

The town held a fandango every night to celebrate their freedom from the outlaws. Grateful residents poured much mescal and other homemade potions of alcohol down Slocum's throat. The festivities were filled with music and dancing that usually lasted until dawn. So his waking hours to work on Marcia's project proved to be very limited. Construction went slowly. The postholes proved unyielding. However, with some blisters and cussing, the holes were finally drilled and posts set. Then he put up the top poles and lashed them together so it looked like a skeleton.

He was facedown sound asleep when she shook his shoulder.

"Yes?" he mumbled, without opening his eyes to the piercing light.

"There are two men at the plaza asking for you."

"Lawmen?" He raised up on his elbows, at once awake and considering who they might be.

"Bounty men. I think."

"What are their names?"

She shook her head. "I didn't hear that. No one has told them that you are here. I swear, no one—"

"I know that, but those men could hurt someone trying to get to me." He sat up and began to pull on his boots. "What do they look like?"

"Texicans. They have leather cuffs and bull-hide chaps."

"Probably are Texans." One thing he knew by her description—they were not the Abbott brothers. The Abbotts usually wore brown suits and tried to act like they were real lawmen.

"What can I do?" she asked.

"We need to send them north. Across Polonski's Bridge and up into that country where I came from."

"I will tell them—"

He reached out and caught her arm. "No. You have the bartender tell them that he thinks I rode that way."

"But—"

"They won't get mad at him for they will think he didn't really know. But you they might come back and punish when they learn the truth."

"You won't leave now, will you?"

"Not until dark," he said.

"Good. I want to send some food with you."

"I'll be here when you return."

Damn, damn, something all the time. No doubt that worthless Yarborough had sicced the bounty men on him. He owed Yarborough for doing that. Probably ran into those rannies down in Santa Fe and sent them thundering up to Benito. Four to five days—he'd had enough time. Slocum hated to leave Benito, Marcia's warm company and soft bed, but the word was out and he'd best make tracks. Stop off in Santa Fe, play a few hands of poker, fill his pockets again, and hit the trail south.

Dressed, he went and saddled the bay to have him ready. Reshod and rested, the pony should travel well. Slocum felt itchy to be moving, but first he wanted those bounty men headed off to the north. If they had never seen him, then he would be safe, for the blurry drawings on those Kansas posters had little resemblance to him.

The dogs began barking, and his hand shot to his holster. Juan slipped in the gate. He hurried across the yard, out of breath.

"Those men are riding north. What can I do?"

"Follow them to Polonski's Bridge. See if they go across. If they stop you, just tell them you are looking for a stray horse."

"I'll do that."

"What color is the horse?" Slocum asked.

Juan blinked at him.

"What color is the horse you are looking for?"

"Oh, yes. A bay with Triple T brand on his left shoulder. One cropped ear." The youth smiled broadly. "We are going to be married next year. Theresa and me. Her father wants me to work in the store. You did that for me."

"No. You're a brave man. But don't fight these men. Only see where they ride. I can fight my own wars."

"I will see where they go."

"Thanks, Juan."

Slocum felt much better; if his plan worked, he'd push on to Santa Fe. Charlie Forsyth should be around there; he owed Slocum a hundred bucks. It was an old gambling debt. He planned to collect that as well in the territorial capital.

After dark, Juan returned to report the pair had crossed the suspension bridge headed northwest. Marcia beamed at the news and handed Slocum his saddlebags filled with food to take along.

"When can you return?" she asked.

"I guess I better pay someone to build the remada."

"No, I have money enough to hire workers." She pushed him toward the horse. "Do you have enough money?"

"I'm fine. I have twenty bucks, and I'll turn it into a hundred in Santa Fe. Collect another hundred from this old boy down there that owes me."

She pressed a double eagle in his palm. "This is for good luck."

"I always need good luck." He took her into his arms and kissed her hard. A knot formed in his throat when he released her and straightened. He could live forever in this sleepy valley, wake up every morning to her bright smile. Even help her with the lambing in the early springtime, cut firewood with her in the mountains, irrigate the small fields and pitch the sweet alfalfa hay—but he had to go on. Her muscled stomach, short shapely legs, and rock-hard butt were made for love. Damn, he hated to ride off and leave all that behind.

"Come back to see me—soon," she said.

"I will," he promised, and Juan went ahead to open the gate. The light from the doorway streamed out on them as he mounted up. Her dogs danced around his horse in excitement.

He set his spurs to the bay and loped away in the moonlight, out the long lane past the grapevines of her neighbor that reflected the silver light. Sometimes it was easy to leave a place, sometimes difficult. This was one of the tough ones.

After Slocum crossed the last ridge, he began to catch sight of the church steeple on the Santa Fe Plaza. The back road he traveled wound through the dusty junipers. He was not anxious to bust into town and tell everyone he was there. For one thing, Yarborough might be licking his wounds in the vicinity. Slocum planned to avoid that bully until he could even the score for sending those bounty men up to Benito. That revenge would be sweet someday.

His eyes ached from being up for a night and a day in the saddle. The bay was tuckered out. Slocum turned up the dry wash to a small, familiar hovel and dismounted heavily.

A sleepy-faced woman clutching a blanket to her throat looked at him in disbelief. "That you, Slocum?"

"It ain't the sandman," he said, and stripped the latigos loose on his girth.

"You've been riding hard?" She straightened. Obviously she had nothing else on but the blanket.

"Sorry I woke you. Can I put him in the corral?"

"Sure, sure, you know you're always welcome here. Bock is gone."

"Far away?"

"Three years."

"What for?" He frowned at her. That was prison time she spoke about. He hitched the horse, and followed her inside to hear the rest of her story.

"Shooting some damn pilgrim. They got into it during a card game. Lucky they didn't hang him. The pilgrim had rich kinfolks back East. Boy, they really raised hell. It was self-defense."

"He have a lawyer?"

"Public lawyer. Some scared sumbitch was afraid of his

shadow. I mean, Bock almost had his neck stretched."

"Damn, girl, I'm sorry."

"It's hard to go back to the street." She slung the blanket away and took hold of the straight-back chair. Her tall, thin figure looked appealing. The teardrop breasts still shook.

"I wish I'd known," he said.

"Nothing anyone could do. The prosecutor threatened Bock's lawyer he'd have him disbarred if Bock got off. The jury should have had the guts to turn him loose. The dude was armed, even had his gun out. Bock shot first, but the dead man's folks had money and you know what money will buy."

"Sorry, Sal. Hey, you were sleeping. Go back to bed. I'll put the pony up, come back, and do the same thing."

"You always were my favorite man, Slocum." She forced a smile for him. "There's some food—"

"Go to bed. I can find it. Besides, I been up a day and a night and sleep sounds wonderful right now."

"Gawd, I wish Bock was home. Wish he could see you. He loved you, Slocum."

"I did him the same way. Go to bed." He pointed toward the bed in the corner of the small shack.

She gave a shrug and obeyed him. He went back outside, took the horse around back, and put him in the corral. The hay in the bunk was old, sun-bleached, but he promised the pony he'd get him something better after he slept a few hours.

Back inside, she was curled up in a fetal knot on top of the mattress. Sal always had the smallest ass. He toed off his boots, hung his holster on a chair that he dragged close to the bedside, removed his shirt and vest, then lay down on his side of the bed. In minutes he fell asleep.

It was dark outside. For a moment he was unsure where he was at. Then he recalled Santa Fe, Bock's place, and Sally— someone was undoing his belt buckle and bucking up and down on top of him.

"Damn you, Slocum," she swore.

"What's wrong now?" he asked.

"You were supposed to come to bed without any clothes on."

"So?"

"Help me get them off."

"What for?"

"What for? I'm going to give you what for if you don't help me get them off."

"I thought you and Bock—"

"Bock ain't been here in nine months. I want someone to love me who cares. Even if you don't care, gawdammit, act like you do."

He pulled her down on top of him and kissed her hard. When she came up for air, she swept the hair back from her face and grinned in the darkness at him. "Get those damn pants off. I can't wait a damn minute longer."

There was no need to rush around in Santa Fe—nightlife went on until dawn and beyond. When they finished, she jumped up and excused herself with a sweet kiss for him. She had to go to some fandango, didn't know how long she would be gone. She doubted she would have any overnight visitors at the shack, so he could come back and use the bed with or without her.

Later, on foot, he made his way down to the Elephant Saloon and eased inside the bat-wing doors, looking carefully around under the kerosene lights for a familiar face. Nothing looked out of place, and he slipped back to the card tables. In a haze of cigar smoke, he made his rounds of the tables, nodding to the bar girls who were serving drinks and flirting with the customers.

He found a card game with low stakes, entered it with his thirty dollars, and in three hours found himself broke, except for Marcia's twenty-dollar gold piece. Not a single hand came his way, so he excused himself and went down the street to the Gentleman's Club. He knew a bartender there.

"Howdy. How've you been, Sam?" the man said, knowing full well his name—but "Sam" would do for the moment.

"I'm looking for Charlie Forsyth. He been around here lately?"

"He left a couple weeks ago. He must be down at Bernillia trying to fleece those railroad workers. He owe you too?"

"Yes. He leave some more debts here?"

"Yeah, plenty."

The news was not encouraging, but it meant Slocum better take his horse and ride that way. Gamblers were notoriously rich or poor. If he arrived in Bernillia and found Forsyth with a pot full of money—he could collect with interest.

"Give me a beer."

"I'll buy it. You look down on your heels."

"I am, but I also need to change a twenty-dollar gold piece."

"I can change it and still give you the beer." The man delivered the mug with a large cap of foam on top, and then cashed his gold piece. He intended to leave Sal some of the money. Bad enough she had to go back to working the streets. His vision of Bock in prison made him sick to his stomach. Like his own bad luck—he'd had none at poker, that was for sure. Ready to go, he thanked his friend for the free beer and left by the back way.

Maybe if he caught up with Forsyth at Bernillia, he could at least get some of his money. He hurried up the alley. Come dawn, he needed to be headed south again.

5

The bay horse would never make it. Under the hot sun, Slocum led him on foot. They stopped under the cottonwoods that lined the shallow Rio Grande. Beads of sweat ran down Slocum's face. In disgust, he recalled the cool mountains far behind him. Low moans issued from the animal's mouth, and he started to go down on his front legs. Only a shout from Slocum prevented it. Quickly, he unsaddled the gelding. If it ever went down he'd never get his kack off it. With his gear in hand, Slocum stepped back. The horse closed his eyes, settled down on his front knees, and then sprawled flat on his side, moaning in pain.

Slocum had came too far on him. It branded Slocum's conscience, but the poor beast needed to be put out of his misery. Slocum searched around. There was nothing and no one on the Camino Real highway. He was forty miles south of where the Atchison-Topeka tracks crossed the Rio Grande. And a long ways from Socorro, stuck in the hot desert and on foot. Damn, all his luck was bad.

Slocum used his .45 Colt to put a bullet behind the pony's ear. The animal settled into a quick death. Then filled with disgust, Slocum started down the dusty wagon tracks that served as the road from Sante Fe to El Paso and on to Mexico City. A hot wind singed his face and the ovenlike heat roasted his brain.

Two days before when he'd arrived in Bernillia, he'd looked

37

for Forsyth without any luck, then attended a fandango, where he'd met Alaina Nevarro, a lovely dark-eyed lady whose husband was freighting to St. Louis and had neglected her—or so she'd said. Slocum had boarded the bay with a Mexican family, and they must have fed him some bad hay, or maybe he'd taken distemper, for he hadn't acted right the morning Slocum had headed south.

The hot sun was bearing down on Slocum, and his numb thoughts were all about Alaina's deep feather bed and his regrets over leaving her, when he heard horses and a wagon rumbling toward him. Someone was coming at last—maybe he could hitch a ride with them. Most travelers were friendly.

Two rather large Indian women filled the spring seat. Their mismatched team looked grateful for the rest when the smiling woman reined them up and the two women looked him over.

"You walk to Numbie?" the sober-looking one asked.

"I'm going to Socorro." He nodded toward the south.

"Go to Numbie. Give you burro to ride to Socorro."

Well, that was different, he quickly decided. Where in the hell was Numbie at? He had no idea of the location, but it beat walking, and the idea of a burro even was a lot better than his shank's mare.

Smiley indicated he should get in the back. He agreed, and stowed his gear in the wagon. They were off with a jerk, Slocum seated on the weathered gray boards and bouncing along on his butt. Around him were several handwoven baskets loaded with things in wraps and blanket rolls. Obviously the two women were traveling too. The ride was rough, but it still was better than the alternative.

At midday, they stopped at a grassy place along the river. Smiley spread a blanket on the ground and took a basket from the rig. She indicated he should sit down. Sober Face came back from relieving herself in the willows and joined them on the ground.

A strong hot wind blew out of the south. It rattled the leaves overhead, and at times threatened his felt hat. He was thinking about all his gambling losses in Bernillia as he ate their corn-tortilla-wrapped beans. Smiley gave him another tortilla when he finished. They were spicy and hot.

His poker hands had all turned sour. Even the good ones could not win. He'd left Bernillia dead broke. Alaina had offered him money before he rode out, but he knew Forsyth would be in Socorro, and Forsyth owed him a hundred.

The first night after he left Bernillia, he'd slept along the road. At midday he'd stopped and bought tamales from a woman who lived beside the river. This was his first food since then.

"You plenty hungry?" Smiley teased, handing him another one of her tortillas.

"Plenty. *Muchas gracias.*"

"Bueno," she said.

"What you do in Socorro?" Sober Face asked.

"I'm going there to collect some money."

She nodded in approval and went back to eating.

"How far is Numbie?" he asked.

Smiley looked at her friend for the answer, and she shrugged. With her right hand, she waved south, as if he should know—that way, that far.

"My name's Slocum."

"Her name's Maria," Sober Face said. "My name's Antoinette Regina Bigota Obregeon. They call me Hoop."

"Maria and Hoop. Good." He saved his hat from a gust of wind with his hand. "You have husbands?"

They shook their heads.

"You have wife?" Hoop asked.

"No."

"Good, we get to Numbie, we have big party."

"Fine," he said, a little taken aback—but he sure did not wish to show it, so he stretched. Made no difference to him. With his belly full for the first time in days, and headed south to Socorro by way of their place, he didn't care. He did have some misgivings. With his outrageously bad luck lately, the wagon bed might break in two and dump him on his butt going down the road.

They reached Numbie by dark. It was a small village swept by a strong dust storm. The small unplastered *casa* they stopped at looked bleak. He took out his saddle and leaned into the stinging wind. Hoop opened the door for him and he

piled the saddle inside on the floor. Then he went back and
helped her haul in supplies and their things. That completed,
he went back out and helped Maria unharness. They led the
weary horses around to a pole corral, and she fed them arm-
loads of sweet-smelling grass hay.

Dust cut the visibility down to a short distance. He could
hardly make out the other small hovels nearby. The howling
wind pressed her dress hard to her rounded belly and legs, and
threatened to blow Slocum and Maria away. They fought their
way back, and at last were inside the sanctuary of the small
casa.

He drew in a breath of air, grateful not to be outside. Hoop
motioned for him to take a chair at the table. She had the fire
going in the fireplace, and was busy making tortillas. The wind
whistled at the eaves and whined in song with rising and falling pitches.

Maria lit a small candle lamp in a reflector. Then she went
and found a crock jar. She poured him some liquid in a saucer
and then waited for him to try it.

It was a fair red wine. A little raw, but not bad. He nodded
his approval. Pleased, she filled a cup for herself and Hoop.

"You always lived here?" he asked, sitting back in the high-
back chair.

They nodded.

"Ever been married?"

Maria nodded.

"Hoop's never been married?"

"No. You ever been married?" Maria grinned at him.

"Almost," he said, and laughed. They laughed too.

The wine flowed freely and they all became amused. Maria
wondered where there was a tall enough burro for him to ride
to Socorro. Hoop dismissed her concern—burros were plen-
tiful. Soon she served her fresh tortillas filled with reheated
frijoles and peppers. Night settled in. The candle lamp showed
their enlarged shadows on the wall.

They drank more wine.

"You sleepy?" Hoop asked.

"Some," he admitted.

"Good," she said. "We go to bed."

The bed was a large one and took up a considerable portion of the room. Handmade quilts were folded over the footboard and several pillows were on the head end. Hoop stood up and began to undress.

"You going to sleep in your clothes?" she asked.

"No," he said, feeling easy enough from all the wine that the notion of undressing with two rather portly native women did not bother him.

"You sleep in middle," Hoop said, and he agreed.

The wind calmed down sometime during the night. Sandwiched between two mountains of brown flesh, and worn out by his earlier attentions to both of the sisters, he studied the dark ceiling until his leaden eyelids closed.

He awoke to the smell of coffee. He could not recall the last time he'd smelled fresh-ground and brewed coffee. Perhaps at Alaina's house in Bernillia. It set his teeth on edge. Maria was making flour tortillas, and he quickly dressed.

"Where is Hoop?" he asked, pulling on his boots and grateful they did not expect a repeat performance from him.

"Gone to find you a burro."

"Good." He went outside to relieve his bladder. Standing beside the house pissing, he could hear the morning doves cooing. The wind was calm, but the coolness of the desert in the first light of morning made him shiver. His luck wasn't all bad; maybe Hoop would find him a burro to ride.

He paused before going inside. Hoop came leading a good-sized white burro with a string around his neck up the steep hill from the irrigated land that joined the river.

"Here is your burro," she said, and drew a deep breath.

"Who does he belong to?"

"No one owns a burro. They just use them."

"But I need to got to Socorro."

She shrugged. "When you are done with him turn him loose. Someone else will need him and maybe they will ride him back to here or maybe another person will bring a new burro when they come."

He now understood burro ownership or usage in New Mexico. Grateful for her efforts, he smiled at her, then took the long-eared beast back and put him in the corral until he was ready to leave. The jackass brayed at him loudly when he headed back for the house. Riding a burro was hardly more than a step above walking. Still, in Socorro he had money coming to buy a horse, something he needed very desperately.

He hugged and kissed the sisters good-bye after breakfast. They packed him some food, and he put it in his saddlebags. Then he thanked them. They stood together in front of their *casa*, Hoop wearing a grin to match Maria's. They invited him to come back when he was close to Numbie. He promised he would, and swung aboard his burro with a good-bye.

No one said burros did not buck. Slocum left the little village, the animal crow-hopping and Slocum trying to hold his head up and cussing him.

"Damn you, Whitey, quit that!" In a half run, half buck, he headed south down the Camino Real, bound for Socorro, riding a green-broke jackass, without a penny in his pocket and hoping for better luck. He considered again the picture of the two rotund sisters in the buff, one on each side of him and both of them expecting him to satisfy them. His luck had to get much better. He whipped Whitey into a bone-jarring trot.

6

Two days later he arrived in Socorro. Manuel Mendez lived on a small farm north of the town in the river bottoms where for generations his family had irrigated their patch of land. Deep green patches of alfalfa, beans, corn, and melons filled the small fields. Slocum rode Whitey up the dusty lane beside the ditch of water destined for someone's thirsty field.

"Señor Slocum," Martinia Mendez shouted, and left her wash to run out and hug him. Her very pregnant belly pressed hard against him, and she drew her face up to smile at him.

"Where's Manuel?"

"In the mountains, mining," she said, and gave a toss of her scarf-wrapped head to the towering range to the west. She was a small woman, and even pregnant, her body held its well-proportioned shape.

"Is he not farming?" Slocum asked. The man had made a good living growing and selling dry beans and alfalfa hay to the many freighters.

"No one here has any money to buy anything," she replied. "Manuel is earning some to pay for our water. Come, you must be hungry, you look tired."

"It has been a trying time to get here."

"I saw you came on a burro." She tried to suppress her amusement.

She would laugh harder than that if she knew the whole truth about his ill-fated journey. The two fat sisters were just a portion of the things that had befallen him since he'd come down off the Rockies into New Mexico looking for some peace and quiet.

"Where can I put the burro?" he asked.

"In the corral."

"Thanks. I'll do that."

"Good. I will put out a pan of water for you to wash with. Come along, children," she said to the two little ones close to her skirt.

He unsaddled Whitey and turned him into the corral. At the moment he was not ready to lose his only transportation. He hoped if he found Forsyth, the man would have his money for him. Perhaps when he collected it, he could help Manuel pay his water bill. Slocum and Manuel had done some scouting together for the army, and when Slocum was in the valley, he always stopped by to see the man and his pretty wife Martinia.

He washed his hands and face outside behind the house away from the hot cutting wind. Another dust storm was brewing. He could see great brown clouds rising in the south like a great wall. Damn.

"Better bring your saddle and rifle into the *casa*," she said when he stepped inside. "There are many thieves around these days."

"Oh?"

"Times are very hard and there are many who would steal your teeth if you left them out."

They both laughed, and he went back for his gear. Things must be real tough in this community; always before, anyone else's property was considered scared. He had heard in Bernillia that the Atchison-Topeka had stopped building track because of financial troubles. They'd quit barely across the Arizona line, somewhere short of the Little Colorado. They supposedly couldn't get financing in New York, and many of the men who worked on building the right-of-way had come home to Bernillia. More bad luck.

His gear inside, he sat at her table and teased the children. Martinia rose at the first blast of the storm outside and quickly closed the doors.

"Things are bad enough, but these dust storms are worse, I think," she said, resting her shapely butt against the back door and catching her breath.

He agreed.

She scolded the children for bothering him, but he dismissed her concern. They were pretty babies and handsome as their parents. The little girl and boy were hardly past crawling, and clambered over him as if he was someone they loved. He rather enjoyed them. Manuel was lucky.

"Those men from Kansas . . ." she said, setting a plate of beans and tortillas before him.

"Yes, the Abbott brothers still ride my trail."

"What will you do here?"

"Collect some money a man owes me. You haven't heard if a man named Forsyth is in town?"

"No, I seldom go into town nor do I hear much out here."

"No problem. I'll go to the saloons tonight and find him."

"Will you stay long?"

"Why?"

She chewed her lower lip as if hesitant to ask him something. Then at last she spoke. "I have a couple of fat goats that a man owes me for hay. And I am—well, clumsy." She dropped her gaze down to her belly.

"You need them butchered?"

"*Sí.*"

"Get the goats. I can do that for you."

"Oh, *gracias*. That would be so fine. The children and I have eaten beans for a long time now. Some roasted *cabrito* would taste so good. Tomorrow I will go get them."

"Yes, we will have a feast." He enjoyed her frijoles and fresh tortillas. When darkness came, he would walk to town. The burro was hardly suitable to ride up there. Wait till dark and then hike into town. He was in no hurry, so long as he found his man and collected.

He took a siesta on his bedroll, and when he awoke the wind still tore at her house. Air inside the small room was stale. The swirling dust outside was a deep brown curtain that cut off vision from the small window. It would blister the eyes of anyone who was out in it. Its high-pitched whines and cries made a revenge-filled song. Martinia rose on the bed, stretched, and then smiled at her sleeping children.

At the table, he took his .45 apart and cleaned it. He had not taken the time since shooting the horse, and the fact had niggled him. Spent gunpowder was the metal's worse enemy, and he busied himself reaming out the barrel and cylinder. With the parts scattered before him, he passed the afternoon under her scrutiny.

"What if this man does not pay you?" she finally asked.

"I had thought about that," he said, reassembling the revolver.

"And?"

"I'll just have to kill him." And he pointed the cylinder-less frame at the wall and quietly said, "Bang."

"You know the Brown brothers who did much freighting? They always bought our hay. They have been taken over by the bank in El Paso. They still owe us for it. That is why Manuel went to find work in the mines."

"They were big freighters too?"

"Yes, they were big businessmen. Some say the banks will fail here. Too many cow men have lost their cattle in this drought and the price is no good."

"Things are in a mess. But this man better have my money."

Tears began to slip down her olive cheeks. He motioned for her to come to him. She rose and, sobbing, went around. He sat her on his lap and held her lightly in his arms.

"Oh, I miss Manuel so much. I am so—big. Oh, Slocum, I am sorry—but I am so sad. We were doing so good here."

"You will again."

"I should not be crying on you." She sobbed and shook in his arms.

"Cry all you want, girl. Things are bad now, but they'll get better, they always do."

"But when?"

He didn't have the answer for her. He patted and held her. Poor woman, she tried to be brave, but the bottom had fallen out of her entire life with her so very pregnant, her husband off working in some dangerous mine, and not hearing from him. Things were very rough in her small world.

"Thank you," she said, and wiped her wet eyes on the sides of her small hands. He helped her off his legs. "I needed to do that, I guess."

"We all need to do that at times like this."

"What will happen to everyone?"

"Things will get better, you will see. Manuel will come home and things will be fine again."

"I hope so."

The wind calmed down again after dark, and he hiked to town. It was further than he'd first imagined it, and he found the hitch racks emptier than he'd expected.

Few horses were tied at them, and there was no laughter from the saloon girls nor melodies from the tinny pianos in any of the saloons. He could hear loud crickets outside when he parted the doors of the Lone Star. Two men stood behind the bar. The gaming tables were empty.

"You seen Charlie Forsyth?" Slocum asked the first bartender.

"Who?" the man asked.

"Charlie Forsyth. Never mind, I'll check up the street."

"Nope, I never heard of him."

The Dancing Horse looked equally deserted when he entered it. The bartender recognized Slocum.

"You need a drink? You look bad."

"Couldn't afford water." Slocum looked around with a sigh. His hopes of finding his man flush with any money looked bleaker by the minute.

"I could trade you a couple of drinks for swamping out the place. Dumping the spittoons."

"I may consider it. Right now I need to check some more. You haven't seen Charlie Forsyth?"

"Not in several days. Why?"

"He owes me money."

"Gawdamn, he owes everyone in Socorro money too. Guess you can stand in line."

Slocum narrowed his eyes at the man. Was he telling the truth? Forsyth was that bad off? Slocum had ridden one horse to death and a jackass the rest of the way to learn that the man was busted? Suddenly he slapped his forehead. The man must have lost his good senses. Forsyth always had more things than gambling working for him. Slocum wanted to cry. The worthless bastard needed to be shot in the belly and die the hard way.

"I'll take that damn job swamping. Pour me a double."

Hours later, the sleepy-sounding Martinia opened the door for him.

"You find your man?"

"Nope, but I did learn one thing."

"What is that?"

"Forsyth's as broke as the rest of us."

"Oh, no. Did you shoot him?"

"No, couldn't find the sumbitch."

She hugged him hard in the darkness of the small house. "I am so sorry, Slocum."

He held her tight and rocked her. "Nothing you can do about it." Nothing at all, but if she wasn't Manuel's wife, he knew exactly what he would do with her.

He slept on the floor, despite her offer for him to share the bed with her and the children. For a long time, he lay awake and wondered what he should do next. Somehow he must trade for a horse to ride. That white burro wouldn't outdistance the Abbott brothers' horses. Maybe they were still in Colorado. He could only hope they were that far away.

Daybreak came too early. He rose and went out to relieve himself. He checked on the tail-switching jackass, and fed him some sweet-smelling alfalfa. Then he stood and listened to the song of the morning doves and drew in the cool fresh air that refreshed him. The hulking mountain range to the west might offer him some escape if necessary. It towered above the scattered settlements down in the valley—a great barrier that kept the warlike Apaches to the west, though they had made raids on this side, especially higher in the mountains on small ranches and travelers.

Most of them were on reservations. The few Broncos were hiding in Mexico. He headed back for the house. Apaches or no Apaches, he needed to get over that range and on his way.

"Who has a saddle horse for trade?" he asked her.

"What would you trade for one?" She smiled and brought

him some scrambled eggs and peppers with flour tortillas.

"A good .44/.40 Winchester?" That was about all he could part with. It would be a good swap for a decent saddle horse. It might even give the other fella a better deal. A rifle could bring money and a horse had to eat.

"I will speak to Francisco. His boy has a good horse."

"I would hate to take a boy's horse."

"But then they could go up in the mountains and shoot deer and have food if they had a rifle."

He nodded that he understood.

"Will you watch the children?" she asked. "I am going for the goats."

"Sure." They were no problem.

Slocum sat on the floor and wrestled and played with them. Before long, he heard the bleating. She appeared in the doorway looking a little windswept.

"I have them."

He and his wards went out to inspect the new goats. The little girl wanted to pet them, the boy wanted to ride them. Slocum went back inside and sharpened the knife he kept in his left boot. The edge soon became thinned enough, and he went out to find her.

"Just one today," she said, and led the children away from the scene.

Quickly he separated the brown one from the spotted one and led it pleading away from the pen. He delivered it unconscious with a sharp rap to the head with hammer, cut its throat, and let it bleed out hanging from cross-rail where Manuel must have butchered. Then, taking care not to get hair on the carcass, he began to skin it out, stripping the hide away, the intestines pouring out with the skin that peeled off the hot body.

She quickly came with a pan and recovered them.

"It will be fine there," she said of the carcass, checking the sky for another dust storm—but it was too early for that to start. "I checked about that horse. Francisco and his boy are coming to trade."

About that time, Whitey broke into some loud braying. Good.

The horse was a bay gelding about three years old and obviously trained by the boy who rode him. He called him Bosque. It was with much pride that he showed Slocum how well he reined and even backed.

"How much for the horse?" Slocum asked.

"Times are hard, Señor" said Francisco. "But the boy has done a good job with him, no?"

"Good job, but the horse is a little small for a man."

"But he is *mucho* tough. He's a mustang. He has the blood of the king's horses in his veins. He's a mountain horse. Why, he could go over those Gallinas Mountains like that." Francisco snapped his fingers.

"I am a poor man. I rode in on a burro I am so poor," Slocum explained.

"Is he your burro?"

Slocum shook his head. "No, I borrowed him up at Numbie."

Francisco nodded that he understood and approved. It was not a burro to sell or trade. It was not his, but only borrowed.

"I would trade a Winchester rifle to the boy for his horse," Slocum said.

"Are there any bullets? If he had that rifle he could not afford ammunition. But if he had shells for it, then if he shot a deer, he could trade some of the meat for more bullets. Do you see?" the man asked.

"There are bullets."

"Then we will trade. What will you do with the *blanco* burro?"

"You can use him."

"Good. We will need him to carry home the deer we will kill."

Slocum had a horse at last, and put him in the pen. They took the braying Whitey away with them, and the good Winchester with a near-full box of ammo. Watching them leave with both burro and gun, he hoped he didn't live to regret giving up the repeater.

"So." Martinia smiled at him. "You have a good horse to ride."

"I have a good small horse. Here, I'll carry that carcass up there."

He studied her shapely backside as they headed back for the house, the goat carcass slung over his shoulder. He figured that Manuel must miss her too. He would.

7

During the day he rode the bay up in the foothills to try him out, but never saw any game. He wanted to get Martinia a deer to eat, and planned to shoot it with his .45. In range it was an effective knockdown weapon. The few antelopes he spotted were beyond even rifle range, so he jogged the bay home. Bosque would be all right. What the mustang lacked in height he made up in heart. The next day, Slocum made a wider circle, and spent that night in the mountains. When he rode back to her place the next morning, he felt better about his trade.

He didn't take the horse to town that night. Instead he walked. His hopes were to find Forsyth and collect even a portion of his hundred. The threat of some desperate out-of-work cowboy wanting to go back to Texas and stealing Bosque was serious enough for Slocum to leave him at home.

Full of Martinia's flavorful mesquite-smoked *cabrito*, he made the walk easily. No one looked familiar in the first saloon, and he went on to the Dancing Horse.

"Hey, Slocum. Forsyth was in here asking about you today," the bartender said, busy polishing a glass. "Said that he wanted to see you."

"He say where he was staying?"

"Nope. But he left here and sent a telegram."

"He did?" Slocum leaned closer to the bartender, who motioned him over to the bar.

"They ain't supposed to tell things like this, but the telegraph man's a friend of mine. Forsyth sent a telegram to some fellas in Santa Fe, and they weren't there."

"And?"

"They must have already left Santa Fe."

"So?"

"Their names was Abbott. They bankers or money men?"

"Gawdamn bounty hunters. Where's that damn Forsyth staying around here?"

"Bounty men?"

"Gawdamn his worthless hide. Where is he hiding?"

"At some whore's place behind the Chinese laundry."

"She Chinese?"

"No. Her name's Melanie or Matty. Where you going in such a rush?"

"To cave his head in. He owes me money and he's sicced some bounty hunters on me for the damn reward."

"Here, have a free damn drink. You need one." He fumbled the glass on the bar, then poured the double shot to the top.

"Guess you'll be dusting out of here after you settle with Forsyth?"

"Yeah, El Paso, tell them."

"Right. El Paso."

Slocum finished the whiskey. It flew down his throat like coal oil and made his ears hot. "I owe you. I'll pay you back someday." He slapped his hand down on the bar and then saluted the man.

"Hey, good luck, Slocum, see you again. Maybe your luck will be better."

"It's better already."

"See ya," the man offered as Slocum hurried outside.

He hit the boardwalk on the run. The two blocks to the Chinese laundry went fast. He went inside. The steamy front area smelled of starch when he entered.

"Help you?" the Oriental with the thin mustache asked.

"I need to find Matty or Melanie. Girl that lives around here."

"Have pretty China doll you likee better?"

"No, I need to find this girl—Matty."

"Go back of shop, cross street—second tent." He held up two fingers. "You want China girl next time. Much better screwee than white girls."

"I bet they do. Sorry, I have no money to pay you." Slocum backed toward the door. He couldn't recall ever being so broke in all his life. He always tipped people like this man for their information.

"You come back, me show you plenty good girls."

"I will first chance I get." He left the laundry and went back into the night. The passageway between the two buildings was dark as pitch, and he wondered if anyone lurked in the shadows. Hand on his gun butt, he eased from the narrow corridor and across the dark street. There was a light on in the second tent.

"Forsyth! You mangy bastard! That's all the money I have!" It was a woman's voice, sharp and shrill.

If that no good double-crosser had any money at all on him, Slocum intended to get it. He crouched down and listened to them talk.

"Them Abbotts get here soon, we'll have all kinds of money," Forsyth said. "They already left Santa Fe, so they must be right on his ass. They weren't there for my telegram, so they must be close to getting here."

"How much did they promise you?" she asked in a whiny voice.

"Two-fifty. I've got to find out where he's staying."

Slocum wondered how he could collect the two-fifty, but the fact that the Abbotts usually didn't pay those bounties stuck in his mind. He'd better settle for the cash in Forsyth's pocket that he'd taken from his hooker. Couldn't be much, but it would be something.

He backed up when he saw the man's shadow on the canvas coming out. Forsyth put on his bowler and started back toward the main street. Slocum skirted around the first tent and soon was on his heels. Before he reached Main Street, Forsyth whirled around as if to trap whoever was following him.

Slocum shoved the muzzle of his .45 in the man's gut and told him, "Shut up! I'm a-warning you, if you make one wrong move, I'll blow you to Hell."

"Slocum—oh, dear God, man, I've been looking for you. I'll have that money for you in a few days. Where are you staying, old friend?"

"Give me the gawdamn money in your pants pocket right now."

"I've had some setbacks."

"And you also wired the Abbott brothers."

"Who said that?"

"You did. I heard you tell that sweet thing back there. They're coming here to get me."

"Oh, no! Slocum!"

Filled with rage, Slocum struck the gambler over the head with his pistol barrel, sent his hat flying, and drove him to his knees. The second blow silenced Forsyth. Slocum holstered the Colt and bent over the prone body. In a minute, he'd emptied Forsyth's pockets. Maybe four dollars in bills and some change. Big robbery, and the sumbitch still owed him ninety-five more. He gave the still body a swift kick for good measure, then started back for Martinia's farm. Next time he and Forsyth met, he planned to collect all of it.

Out of breath from running, Slocum rapped softly on Martinia's door.

"Is that you, Slocum?" she asked in a sleepy voice.

"Yes."

"What is wrong?"

"Those bounty men are here or close."

"Oh, no. Did you get the money he owed you?"

"A little money. I caught up with Forsyth. He's the one called in the bounty hunters on me." He handed the money to her.

"You will need it." She pushed it back at him.

"No, you will need for it the baby."

"I can't take this money. It is all you have." She looked ready to cry as she held the few dollars in her hands.

He refolded her fingers around it. "It's not blood money. He still owes me. Keep it. I will be fine. I have a good horse."

"Where will you go?"

"Into the mountains. But I want them to think I went to El Paso, so if they come by, say El Paso."

"Oh, Slocum." She hugged him and began to cry. "What will I do alone?"

"That damn goat—I'll butcher it." He had almost forgotten the task.

"No. Don't. You have no time."

"I can do it. Get a light and we will have it done."

He hurried to the pen, found the animal by moonlight, knocked it out, cut its throat, and dragged it to the crosspiece. He heard her hurrying with the lamp.

"Sorry you had to run," he said. He looked over at her, concerned, his nose full of the copper smell of blood and goat.

"I am fine," she gasped, and lit the small reflector.

In minutes, under the orange light, he'd skinned it out and she'd caught the innards in a pan. He took it down, the drying blood stiffening his fingers, and carried it to the house. She blew out the lamp and looked around in the starlight.

"I hope I have not made you late."

"I'll be fine. Take care of yourself, Martinia, and all the little ones."

He slung the still-hot carcass on her table.

"I can handle it, *muchas gracias*." She stood on her toes to kiss him.

He washed his hands quickly, took up his saddle, and headed for the bay horse. By sunrise, he intended to be deep in the Gallinas Mountains. The horse snorted at the smell of the slaughtered goat that clung to him, but he spoke softly and it settled down. His hand hit the empty scabbard. He would miss the long rifle—no time for worry. He mounted up and waved to Martinia, standing in the starlight with a wrap on her shoulders for the night's coolness had set in.

He headed Bosque uphill. Passing the row of bars, he drew down his hat. A familiar blanket-butted Appaloosa was tied at the hitch rack alongside a solid-colored horse. The Ap belonged to Lyle Abbott, the eldest of the two bounty hunters. Slocum reined his horse to the darker side of the street and rode on.

He thought about Hoop and Maria, who'd found him a donkey to ride, and Martinia, who'd packed food for him to eat. Someday he would get back and repay them. What did he have, a dollar and half to his name? Damn you, Forsyth. That headache I gave you is only part of what I'll do to you next time we meet. He looked back at the twinkling lights of So-corro and then set Bosque into a trot. They had miles and mountain ranges to cover.

The next day, he slept a few hours under a juniper. Then he started back up the strong grade, skirting small settlements and ranches. The less known about his flight, the better it would work. Perhaps he should go by Della Hughes's place over on the Arizona line. He chewed on rock-hard jerky while he rode—so hard that he had to soften it with saliva to even bite it off. In his fire-less camp, he recalled Della's firm breasts and rock-hard belly. The thoughts of her alone were enough to warm him without a fire. Nearby, Bosque, who needed the rest, grazed through his bits.

Clouds gathered. It would rain somewhere up there that af-ternoon. Be good for the grass—it was brown—but he dreaded traveling in a storm. He took a short nap, then was awakened by ravens calling. He looked hard at his backtrail. Were they telling him something or just scolding him? He tightened the cinch and rode on.

Rain came in cold dollar-size drops. He undid his slicker and managed to get under it. Thunder rolled across the land and blinding lightning flashed in his face. He crossed the vast grasslands, and when he topped the next hill he sent a herd of elk cows and calves dashing away in the gray slashing rain. Like most mountain rains, it would be over in a few hours, he assured himself.

Finally he passed through it, a rainbow appeared, and he looked back over his shoulder. A rider was coming up his backtrail. Who was it? He had not noticed him before, and looked around for someplace to hide and let him pass. The country was wide open.

He rode on, and finally found cover in a small grove of pinyons and junipers on a high rise. Feeling damp and cold from the rain, he considered a fire. The big bank of clouds moved southeast. The grumble of thunder in the distance and the lightning bolts struck across the sky. Slocum kicked out a rotten stump and used the pieces to start his fire. Soon it blazed. He stood, hugged his arms against the chill in the air left by the rain, and watched for the rider.

The man rode up. He looked hard-faced, and nodded to Slocum as if he wanted an invite to step down and enjoy the heat.

"Climb off your horse. The fire's free."

"Too damn cold," the man said, wringing his hands and coming to the heat.

"Guess a man's blood gets thin down in the desert?"

"I ain't been out of these mountains myself. Headed for the TZX. They need some broncs stomped. Work's pretty hard to find right now. Nobody needs you."

"Kind of my experience. Thought I'd do a little prospecting," Slocum said.

"Done that once." The man shook his head. "I'd rather be stomped by a bronc than do that again."

"Guess if we're both riding the same direction we could hitch up."

"Be fine with me."

"You look about as food-rich as I am." Slocum laughed.

"Guess we'll have to let do till we can get to another cook-shack."

"Got some jerky. Tough as hell, but you can chew on it a while and it ain't half bad."

"I got some cheese that's drier than a month-old cow turd in a drought and sure enough the stalest crackers I ever ate."

"How about a trade, my jerky for part of your bait."

"That's a deal."

They rode the rest of the day together, and late in the afternoon the bronc-peeler turned off north.

Neither man exchanged names. The food swap had been made earlier and both had acted pleased. Slocum could see some timber ahead and no one else behind; he short-loped Bosque to the top of the mountain.

Bone-tired, he made camp in the pines and took off his bedroll. He unsaddled and hobbled Bosque. He would turn south somewhere ahead to get to Della's. He wondered if he could retrace the route to her place. It had been two years. She might not be so glad to see him, might have someone else in her bed. Soon he fell asleep.

8

The low-walled cabin tucked in the side canyon made a welcome sight to him. Towering ponderosas timbered the steep slopes. Beyond him lay the corral, a few sheds, some sun-bleached haystacks, and the long narrow meadow of Slatter Hughes's place. Slocum twisted in the saddle and checked his backtrail, adjusting the Colt on his hip. Nothing in sight. He turned around, raised the reins, and set Bosque off in a long jog.

Someone in a divided skirt came out on the porch and shaded her eyes with her hand. Then, with a wide grin, she put her hands on her hips.

"That you, Slocum?"

"It sure ain't the boogeyman," he said, and smiled until his chapped lips hurt. He threw his leg over the seat, stepped down, adjusted his pants, and took a good look at her.

Della Hughes was about thirty and had a shapely figure, the blouse filled by her full breasts, her trim waist accented by the wide belt and the divided riding skirt, the toes of her boots peeking out from below the hem. She looked as good as ever, and took his breath away when she wrapped her arms around him.

"Why, you're like hugging a bear. Hard as a rock," she said, and tossed the light brown hair back from her face, blue eyes sparkling, mouth inviting enough to kiss. She had a small nose she wrinkled whenever she was displeased.

"I smell like one too," he added, holding her tight to him.

"I guess you're on the move?"

"Like usual. I left the Abbott brothers in Socorro a couple days ago." He hoped the pair of bounty hunters had gone to El Paso; he'd left enough clues for them that he planned to go there.

"Those two bastards still after you?"

"Never quit. Tell me about you." He looked down into the depths of her deep blue eyes.

"Good thing you came." She looked a little flush-faced under the deep tan.

"Why's that?"

"I'm having rustler problems and figure you can stop it for me."

"You know who they are?"

She nodded grimly. "Trouble is, they are just boys."

"Give them a good tanning."

"Wish it was that easy."

"We can figure out a cure for them. You have any coffee?" His tongue was about to swell out of his head for a cup.

"I guess you ran out three days ago?" She grinned mischievously, and then laughed.

"Sort of. Let's get some and you can tell me all about this deal."

"Fine. Come on. Damn, Slocum, you never come by and I have missed seeing you." She bumped her hip into his, then with her arm around his waist, half dragged him to the cabin.

Della had lived in isolation since her husband, Slatter Hughes, was killed in a horse wreck. He'd been a man twenty-five years her senior. Two White Mountain Apaches rode up to his cabin one day with a crestfallen captive in her teens. They traded her to Slatter for two sacks of corn, a single-shot rifle, some pots, and four blankets. Slatter knew the Apaches well and existed in peace with them. They allowed him to run his cattle in this high country. The girl stayed on. She never spoke to him of her capture or her past. He never asked.

One day, he suggested they ride over to Alma and get married. She agreed. A Mormon bishop married them, and they rode back the same day, eighty miles round trip. Della began a new life in the White Mountains.

Men passed through this strip of high country. Not many questions were asked about their business or reasons for being there. Some were wanted, some simply searching for themselves. They all found good food and rest. Slatter expected them to pay tribute. Not necessarily money, because it was often short in the pockets of such drifters, but you did your share of work. Haying, wood-chopping, branding, repairs, and more haying. Slocum had passed through there before the bowlegged Texan's death and afterwards. Della was a bright star in the vast land of high country that straddled the Arizona-New Mexico border.

She poured him coffee in a tin cup. It was too hot to cuddle in his hands, and he held it by the handle and watched the willowy sweep of her shapely butt when she took the pot back to the stove. Lots of woman out here all alone.

"Figured you'd found a man by this time," he said, and sipped the hot liquid.

She rattled the lids on the stove, then stoked her fire under the pot. With a wry look of disapproval, she said, "After Slatter and then you, I got awful fussy."

"Surely someone came by worth having."

A wrinkle of her nose and a head shake dismissed the notion. She rejoined him at the table.

"All right. Who's rustling your cattle?"

"The Barlow brothers."

"How many of them?"

"Four. It's a game, I figure. They ride down here like they're elk hunting. You know, bring packhorses and they're just boys. But when they clear out, I'll find a calf sucking one of my cows with their 78 brand on it."

"Kind of brazen, isn't it? How old are they?"

"Oldest must be sixteen, the youngest twelve. They usually ride up here to the place and strut around like yearling bulls. Act like I must be so hard up for a man, they expect me to bed 'em."

"That 78 outfit is way up north." He frowned at what they were trying to pull.

"Sure. They're a long ways from here. They're showing off, proving they're big men."

"How often do they come?"

"Every three months or so. I was expecting them when you rode up."

"You keep a gun handy?"

She shrugged. "I could handle them. I've been here over a decade. Four of those years by myself now."

"Have you ever considered selling out?"

"And doing what? Serving beer in a bar?" She shook her head. "That isn't for me, Slocum. No, they'll plant me here."

"Dangerous place. Apaches, outlaws . . ."

Her hand reached out and caught his forearm. "I had a good teacher—God rest his soul. Slatter Hughes taught me who I was and how to be her."

Slocum nodded and looked around the room. The big bed with the peeled-log-frame headboard looked tempting. There was a blackened hearth built of masonry and round creek stones with a seven-by-eight elk rack over the mantel. Three rifles and a shotgun were handy, and there was a pinto steer hide on the floor before the twin rockers. Homey enough for a tomboy like Della, who spent most of her time outside anyway.

"You want to clean up?" she asked. "The shower's full of water. May be cool, but help yourself."

He knew she meant the sheepherder's bath. A tub on a platform with a ladder to haul the water up and a pull-rope contraption to let the water out in shower form. Sun heat warmed it, and after a day took enough chill from it to make it usable.

"I want to do that after I put my horse up."

"Bet you haven't eaten much lately either, have you?" She turned her face and looked skeptically at him.

"No, I haven't. Seems like there's not many cafes between here and Socorro anymore."

"I've got some venison. I'll cook some for you."

"Thanks." He finished the coffee, rose, and headed out the door to put up his horse. Food, a bath, and the company of a beautiful woman—almost too good to be true. On his long ride from down on the Rio Grande at Socorro to her place, he'd avoided as many places or people as possible. That left fewer clues for the Abbott brothers to follow in case they didn't go to El Paso. That meant a not-so-steady diet of tough jerky, and the crumbly, too-dry cheese and stale crackers he'd swapped the bronc-stomper for.

He looked forward to some venison—about anything cooked would taste good to him. Reins in hand, he led the bay to the corral and undid the latigos. Someone was coming. Out of habit, he shifted the .45 and undid the thong on the hammer.

Three riders appeared. Their horses were not familiar, and he settled a little. He swung the rig off the pony's back and tossed it on the corral fence, then took the blankets off and spread them out to dry. With an eye on the men who reined up before the cabin, he led the gelding in the corral, slipped the bridle off, and started out of the gate.

"Howdy, ma'am," the one with the black beard said. Hat in hand, he leaned over on his big roan horse to speak to her. "Randy's my name, that's Tad and Josh."

Della said something to them and nodded.

"We're a little saddle-weary, ma'am, and could sure use a bite to eat."

"Get down, you can water your horses. I about have some food ready, so don't be long."

"We'll sure do that. Thank you, ma'am." He replaced his hat and gave Slocum a hard look in passing. They exchanged nods and the men rode on.

Randy was in his thirties. A slender man about five-eight. Sharp facial features under the raven-black beard. His put-on tone of voice caught Slocum's ear. As if every word needed to be pronounced and projected or you wouldn't understand what he meant.

Tad was a kid in his late teens, and Josh was a gray-whiskered hardcase. If they weren't on the run, then they were looking for something. Like buzzards circling on an updraft, searching for carrion to grab. They would take any opportunity that didn't resemble hard work.

"Company?" he asked her from the doorway.

"Strangers," she said. "I get them all the time. But you know that."

"Yes. But aren't you ever afraid?"

"Slocum, I haven't been afraid since those Apache bucks brought me here. That was my last day of fear in my life."

He nodded. The only way to survive the harsh grain of this land—don't yield to the threats.

The three washed their hands at the bowl on the porch. Then they filed inside with hats in hand and hung them on the pegs by the door.

"Reckon we haven't met, sir?" Randy offered to Slocum.

"Slocum."

The man stuck out his hand. They shook.

"Nice place you have here, Slocum."

"Not mine, just a friend stopping by."

"Very nice. Oh, that's Tad and Josh."

Slocum nodded to them.

"We've been in Utah. Headed for Mexico," Randy said. "I guess the Apaches are all on the reservation?"

"Don't count on it," Slocum said.

"You mean there's still some up here?" Randy asked over his shoulder.

"There's some," Della said, setting the venison and other food on the table. "Pays to be on your guard. They usually will only steal your horses."

Randy nodded and sat down. The others joined him. Slocum took a seat opposite them.

"My, my, good food," Randy said, and reached for the meat platter. "Boys, this is sure to be a feast this lady has prepared for us."

"Ma'am?" Tad asked. "You live up here alone?"

"Yes. My husband was killed a few years ago."

"And may God rest his soul," Randy interjected, and ducked his head quickly in reverence. Then he busied himself filling his plate.

"My, but it's good," he said after his first forkful of venison. "Wouldn't you agree, Slocum?"

"Cooking is always good here."

"Yes, sir, I heard that. Cooking was always good here."

"You must have talked to some of my other visitors," she said, pouring coffee around the table.

"Yes, ma'am, I did. His name was Snuffy something."

"Snuffy Temple. He's not been by here in a long time."

"Matter of fact, ma'am, he won't be coming by soon either."

"No?" She straightened and looked hard at the man.

"No, he's in the Utah pen for horse taking." Randy busied himself cutting up the meat on his plate. "Has two more to serve."

"That explains why, then. Sorry the biscuits are cold."

"Oh, that's no problem," Randy said, and the other two, busy eating, waved away her concern.

"I guess you've been to Mexico, Mr. Slocum?" Tad asked.

"Several times."

"Be my first trip there."

Della laughed. "They will like you down there." She exchanged a knowing look with Slocum, who agreed in silence. Innocence of youth was something that Mexican women craved. And they knew how to corrupt the likes of him. If white men looked for innocent young women, Mexican females took great pride in introducing innocent males to the pleasures of their bodies.

"A man named Vasquez is hiring us," Randy said, making a point with his fork.

Slocum nodded. The name meant nothing to him.

"Big rancher and he has mines."

The man's purpose in explaining his business held little interest to Slocum. The venison roast tasted wonderful and his mouth exploded with saliva. Good to have real food again. It had been a while. His stay in Socorro, except for the goat, had not brought much good food.

"Someone's coming!" Randy drew his Colt and rushed to the door.

"Don't shoot, for God's sake," Della said, sounding annoyed, and tried to elbow him back. "Until we can know who it is."

Who was it? Slocum couldn't see from where he stood at the table, but she won the front position from Randy and the pair of them blocked the doorway.

9

"It's only Charlie Two Horse," she said.

Randy holstered his gun and came back to the table.

"Come in, Charlie." She waved to a man that Slocum still could not see. Directly, a large-headed Indian under a well-worn felt hat, wearing a blue silk shirt and red neckerchief, came in the doorway.

She introduced the burly man around the room. The man nodded to each, then took the place next to Slocum where she indicated he should sit.

"Charlie brought me two new horses," she announced. "He's a great horse catcher."

Charlie began to fill his plate, and she brought him coffee. The Indian looked perfectly at home, and the others settled back to eating their meal.

"You Apache?" Tad asked.

Charlie nodded.

"You know Geronimo?"

The man nodded.

"Know him well?"

Charlie looked away as if he was figuring out something. "One time he told me if I went up this canyon, there were three wild horses. I could go there and catch them and sell them for money."

"I guess that worked?"

"Yes, but he never told me the man's money was no good."
Charlie shrugged. "Maybe he didn't know."

"What was wrong with it?"

"Countered something." He shook his head in doubt.

"Counterfeit?"

"Yeah."

"So what happened?"

"I paid a man who I owed with it."

"Did he get mad?"

"No." Charlie shook his head quickly. "He was so tight, he
hid it with his other money and never knew mine was the bad
money."

They all laughed. Slocum drew in a strong whiff of campfire
smoke and horse sweat. Charlie needed a bath as bad as he
did. Maybe the three men would ride on after the meal and
he could take one. As quick on the trigger as they were, they
had someone chasing them, or suspected they did.

"Charlie?" Randy began. "What would you charge to guide
us to Silver City?"

The Indian stopped eating. He never looked at the man, just
chewed his food and then said, "Five dollars."

"We'll hire you. How long will it take to get there?"

"Two, three days."

"Make it two and I'll give you two more dollars."

Charlie agreed.

After their meal, Randy paid her with a ten-dollar gold
piece. She offered him change, saying it was too much, but
he dismissed it. She paid the coin to Charlie for the two obviously unbroken horses he had left her. The four cinched up
their saddles, climbed aboard, and with a wave to her and
Slocum, headed south.

"Let's look at my new horses," she said.

The pair was in a back pen by themselves. Slocum walked
around them. Loose, they snorted distrustfully at him and skit-
tered away. One was a tall gray with a long tail that brushed
the ground, the other a snorty chestnut with lots of white
around his eyes.

"What will you do with them?" he asked.

"Oh, some saddle tramp will drop by and need to rest a few days and he can break them for me."

"He may have come by."

"I wondered about that." She smiled at him, pleased.

"Let me get a bath and a shave." He ran his palm up the side of his beard-stubbled face. "Might smell a lot better to that chestnut even."

She laughed at his words, and stepped off the fence when he came out of the pen. They walked back to the house.

"Slatter's pants should fit you." She looked him over as they went along. "Give me those and I'll wash them while you bathe."

"Right here?"

"You can take them off up there." She motioned toward the shower structure. "Guess I've seen it all before."

"Guess so," he said, and realized his face was red.

He didn't get two more steps until she blocked his way. With the look in her eyes, the set to her mouth, words weren't needed. He bent over, took her in his arms, and kissed her. Flames torched his brain and he wanted her—to possess her body even there in the dirt—but at last better sense prevailed.

"Let me clean up first."

"Sure," she said, but sounded as if her heart was not in waiting. He stuck his hat on her head and put his hand on her shoulder for balance while he toed off his boots.

"I guess those wild horses can wait till in the morning," he said.

She never looked away. "They can."

"I guess neither of us will get much sleep if we go to bed."

"Don't plan to." She gathered his clothes in her arms and left.

His shower proved to be a short one. The water felt like ice and he soaped quickly, rinsed off, and looked around for a towel. He blinked twice. She stood holding a towel, and all she had on was his hat.

"You can shave later," she said, and began to dry him.

"Whatever you say," he told her, with a shiver running up his back.

He gingerly walked barefoot to the house with her. Who

needed clothes anyway? Only the blue jays and magpies could peek at them. With the rough porch boards under his soles, he stole a quick look at the meadow and the rest. Nothing out there in sight. He followed her inside and she closed and barred the door.

Then they raced for the bed. She jumped on top of it and danced around. Her full breasts rose and swayed with her steps.

"Slocum, why have you been gone for so long?"

"I guess business kept me away."

She dropped to her knees, reached out, and squeezed his face in her long calloused fingers. Her soft mouth met his and her hot tongue began to search his teeth and mouth. At last they tore apart and she scrambled to pull the covers back. Then quickly she slid down in the bed on her back, pulling him on top of her. With her eyes glazed over, she smiled at him.

"I can't wait a minute longer." She drew her knees up high and rubbed her heels on the outside of his legs and butt.

He reached down, parted her moist gates with his fingers, and lowered himself on top of her. His hips ached to plunge deep inside, but he wanted it to last. Slowly he began to probe her. She threw her head back and moaned for more. Her tight belly rose and she strained for all of him until their pelvises smashed together.

His full-blown erection, a ballooned stick of dynamite, was ready to blow her apart. Her contractions began to ruthlessly strip it. His breath raged in and out of his throat, and her desperate pleas and sighs matched his own drive. As desperately as he sought her, she fought back for him. With his arms he gathered both her legs into the air, then folded her up and began to furiously pump her with wild abandon. At last he issued a scream and exploded in a shower of stars. Numb and pressed hard to her, he let her legs slip down, and they both collapsed in a pile of withered exhaustion. Then still coupled, they lay side by side and closed their eyes, still dizzy from the wild ride.

They napped. Then he awoke, stroking her firm breast; she tried to snuggle closer and they came apart. She began to gently pull on his half-hard dick, and it began to stiffen. He rose on top of her, and she hugged him to her. Their mouths met. In a few minutes he was back inside her. This time they savored the movements and dreamily he pumped her. She locked her feet behind his back and raised her stomach up to meet him. Damn, what pleasure. He rested deep inside her. But she was unsatisfied and with a foxy grin, reached underneath to gently squeeze his scrotum.

He pushed deeper and deeper each time, until at last in the very bottom with her crying "yes," he came and they fell in another numb heap. He drew a deep breath and considered his good fortune. With her ripe form in his arms, he went to sleep.

In the darkness, he awoke and discovered her head on his stomach. She was on her hands and knees, and her hot mouth encircled his prick in a frenzy. Half asleep and shaken, he arched his back for more. Damn. She tore her face away, gripped his prick with her hand, and then scurried up until she was over him. She eased herself down. He took the nearest breast and began to suck on the nipple. It flared hard under his tongue, and she began to bounce on his stomach in wild abandon.

What was that noise outside?

The horses were out. They both froze. She spilled off him and he was out of the bed in a bound, grabbed a rifle from the rack, and levered a shell in the chamber on the way. She fought the bar out of place, and he ran out on the porch into the darkness. Too late. The shouts of Apache bucks shattered the starlit scene. With a drum of hooves they raced off into the night with her saddle stock and his pony.

They'd got them all. He stood barefoot on the rough-hewn porch boards and caught his breath.

"Stinking bastards stole the horses."

She hugged him from behind and dreamily laid her face on his back. "Guess we're lucky to be alive. Must be young bucks. They never did that before."

Like the farmer said when the mule died, he never did that before. Well, Slocum had been in worse messes than this one. He turned and hugged her with his free hand. She pressed tight to him, and he savored her smooth skin and warm body against him.

The chill of the night swept his bare skin. He drew in his breath with a shiver and herded her back inside. Nothing they could do until daybreak. Those damn renegades had not only taken their horses, but they'd interrupted a perfectly lovely moment—they owed him.

10

In the early morning light, he stood on the corral fence and viewed their good fortune. The Apaches hadn't taken either the gray or the chestnut. Somehow, in their haste and the darkness, they'd stolen her six saddle ponies and Bosque, but failed to get the green ones in the herd.

"I know they were by themselves in that pen on the other side, but I wonder why they left them," she said, peering through the rails.

"Didn't take the time. Apaches hate the night. To get killed at night means to an Apache that you walk the land of never-never or something bad like that and don't ever get inside heaven."

"They're very superstitious," she said, straightening up and putting her hands on the top rail. "But damn, those old ponies of mine were getting some age on them. That's why I ordered two new ones. Plus I sell and trade for some horses." She wrinkled her nose at him.

He knew what she meant. She sold some to riders on the run who passed through her place with their horses worn out. It was a profitable business. The ones the Apaches stole had probably been taken in trade and were either stove-up or wind-broke. Slocum always wondered about Slatter Hughes and why he chose to live up there so far from everyone. He too might have been a man on the run from something.

"You aren't mad at me?" she asked in a little voice when they headed back for the house.

"Why?"

"I kind of lost my mind last night. . . ."

He reached over and hugged her. "You can do it again."

"Yeah, and maybe the Apaches won't steal the rest of our horses. Come on, let's get some breakfast and then we can see how those horses ride."

They hurried for the house. He shaved, and she made them biscuits and gravy to serve with her venison. The smell of her cooking while he worked the straight-edged razor over his face made his empty stomach roil and churn. Three square meals a day might kill him. He looked close into the smoky mirror to scrape the lather and stubble from his upper lip. Finished, he rinsed his face with handfuls of water, and cleaned up the rest of the soap with a towel.

"You look much better. Why do men think beards make them look so manly?"

"Damned if I know. Feels better to be free of them."

"You better sit down and eat. I figure those two ponies are head twisters." She wiggled her head around like a bronc caught in a lariat. Then she raised up and tied her own mane back with a leather thong. "They will be fun to break in a hurry."

"Just horses," he said matter-of-factly.

Biscuits hot from the oven, more sliced venison, and a cast-iron skillet on the table filled with pepper-speckled gravy made his mouth water. A beautiful woman, a good cook, and interesting company all rolled up in one at a sit-down meal. What more could a man ask for? He didn't know, and pitched in.

After breakfast, they went back to the corrals and observed the pair. Horses had minds of their own. Luke Stufflefield had taught him that notion. That skinny horse breaker could dance a lariat around any running pony's head and know in a glance how hard that one would be to convince. Slocum recalled many of those lessons when he stepped in the pen and shook out a loop.

The pair divided and he sunk a noose around the gray. Took a hitch on the center post and went walking up the rope, talking to him. Wide-eyed and stomping his front foot, the gray tried to figure which way he could bolt and escape. The rope was not tied hard and fast to the post. The gray blew rollers out his nose and backed his neck against the constrains of the rope, which would cut off his wind if he continued to stiffen.

"Watch him, he's going bolt at you," she warned.

Slocum held up his hand to silence her. If the gray did that, then he would move, but for the minute the horse's reaction was one of frozen fear. He let the animal smell his hands, the whole time talked soothingly to him. Then he began to work them over him, first his neck to show him there was nothing to fear, and then going back further and talking to him when the fear welled up ready to burst. In a few hours, he saddled the gray and tied up his right hind foot.

The chestnut proved much easier to settle. Within an hour, he wore a saddle and Slocum was riding him around the pen. Della called him to lunch, and he left both horses saddled and tied.

"You're easy on horses," she commented, refilling his coffee cup.

"No need to have a fit. Most bronc-busters usually feed their own ego. Besides, you have to outthink a horse."

"I like it," she said with a grin. "I'm anxious to ride the chestnut. He looks gentle."

"He'll be fine. The gray will too. I'll shoe them tomorrow and we should have riding stock."

"Funny thing," she said, standing with her back to him at the stove. "Apaches have never stolen anything from here before. I have given them food and blankets, but they always came and asked before."

"Things are more desperate for the Bronco Apaches. The army is paying for their heads now."

"Oh." She shivered in disgust.

"Hard ways for hard people." He understood their plight and their desperate flight from persecution. He too had to flee, always looking over his shoulder. It was a hard way to exist day in and day out.

"It is," she said. "Slatter always had a way with those people. They understood each other. The older ones still stop by and see me."

"The troublemakers are probably going to Mexico and needed fresh horses to go there." He rose and nodded to her, ready to go back to his horse-breaking. "You're going to fatten me."

"It wouldn't hurt," she said, and dried her hands. "I'm coming too."

By late afternoon, he was riding the gray. The trip was not as easy as with the chestnut, but he managed to control the situation and never let the horse buck. Clouds were gathering, and there was thunder over the peaks to the south. He expected it to storm any time. Then in the corner of his eye, he spotted something on the mountainside.

"Someone's coming," he said, and stepped off the gray. Out of the timber across the meadow came three hatless riders descending the steep slope. They all wore red headbands, so he knew they were army scouts. Perhaps he knew them personally.

"Scouts?" She stood on her toes to see them.

"Yes."

"I'll go get them some fried apple pies," she said, and hurried for the house.

They came in a long trot, and he met them.

"What brings the military here?" he asked.

The head scout, a handsome Apache boy, said, "Loco is on the warpath. He and thirty warriors came up from Mexico to get more men to go with him."

"They stole seven horses from us last night."

"Commander said you should go to town," the scout said, acting pained.

"Which town?" Slocum asked. It was sixty miles to anything that resembled a town.

The scout shrugged. "Maybe go to Alma."

"You thank the commander. She's lived here a long time in peace with your people."

"But Loco is mad. He will not honor the old ways."

"I understand." He turned to watch Della hurry from the cabin with her plate of food for the scouts.

"Here, I have some fried pies for you," she said, and handed them to each of the mounted scouts. Her efforts put broad smiles on their brown faces. She knew what Apaches liked. They nodded in approval.

"Tom Horn still work with you scouts?" Slocum asked, recalling an old friend from his days as a scout.

"Good man," the head scout said, and nodded between bites.

"Tell him Slocum said hello."

"Slo-cum."

"Yes."

"Tell him good when we get back." The scout reined his horse around to speak to her. "Plenty good apples. You and him must go to town. Loco is very angry."

"We will watch for him," she said, and the scouts nodded approval to her and headed north.

After the threesome left, she turned to Slocum. "Should we leave?"

"I guess he knows more about Loco than we do. I'll get the horses shod. It might not hurt to ride over to Alma and see. Why, Loco could be anywhere by now." He wondered if he was taking too many chances staying there another night. But green, unshod horses would never make it to Alma.

"It's fixing to rain here." She pointed to the approaching thunderhead.

"Yes, I'll put some slickers over those saddles and you get to the house."

"Don't get struck by lightning." She raced for the porch. The drum of the downpour roared up the narrow valley. He tied a slicker over each of the saddles and spoke to the horses. To leave them tied and saddled through the afternoon thunderstorm would only add to their education. Big dollar-size drops of cold rain pelted him in his dash for the door.

He rushed inside laughing. She quickly hugged him and their mouths met. After a few minutes of near-breathless kissing, she slipped out of his arms and quickly barred the door, then looking smug, crossed the room to stand before him.

"Can't break horses. Guess we can do some riding of our own."

"I'm game," he said, and they began to undress in a fury.

Clothes soon littered the floor. Unbuttoning his underwear, he admired the turn of her shapely hip and caught his breath.

Outside, the wind drove the rain hard at the shingles. Thunder rolled up and down the valley, and lightning illuminated the cabin with dancing bright flashes. A brutal storm—the horses would learn all about being tame after this dose of weather.

A chill in the room caused gooseflesh to run up his arms when he held her naked form. When her warm body pressed against his, he knew the ride would be as wild as the weather. They dove in the bed and were under the covers in seconds.

11

He slipped from the house before dawn. Apaches liked sunrise for their surprises. He had a well-oiled Spencer of Della's in his hands. He regretted the trade of his Winchester .44/.40, a much more effective repeater with a longer range, but without the trade he might have been in the grasp of the Abbott brothers. He still raged at the thought that Forsyth had double-crossed him.

The birds were awakening. He slipped along the front of the cabin and headed for the corrals. His senses were alert and ready for anything. The two horses were still in the pen. He eased around and checked out the saddle shed and the haystacks. No sign of anything out of place. Then he paused as the purple sky turned pink and dawn peeked from over the rim.

He'd best take her to Alma until things settled down. The whole U.S. Cavalry must be out looking for Loco. "Loco is mad." The scout's words rang in his ear.

After breakfast, he shod the ponies. They tried to fight it, but with persistence, he nailed plates on them. The entire time he kept the Spencer handy. She fixed food for them to eat on the way, then made a bedroll up for her own use, and he laced it on behind her saddle.

He tied the sack of food to his saddle horn and she closed the cabin door.

"I sure hope it's here when I get back," she said, sounding uncertain.

"Good chance it'll be. Loco don't hate you."

"You never know who he hates and what he will destroy on a raid like that."

"I'll help rebuild it if he does destroy it."

"You could stay here permanently."

He shook his head. "No, they'd find me. In the days when Slatter first came here, they'd never have found this place, but nowadays, they'd hear about me and come up here in no time."

"I could sure use you. Well, I mean at hay time and gathering cattle."

"I know, but much as I'd like to stay, I can't. Here, watch that pony when you get on him. He isn't really broke to ride, just to put up with you."

They mounted and set out. The green horses acted a little spooky, but they never bucked. They took the trail south. When the horses settled down he told her to make her mount trot, and they hurried on.

It was a column of smoke in the sky that he noticed first. A plume of it—something was burning, not woods or meadow, but a building. He wanted her to stay back and he would go see about things, but she refused to be left and they headed for the source.

"It's Dulcie Strong's place," she said.

"You know her?"

"Yes. She's a Mormon's wife. Oh, I hope her and the children are all right."

They rode down the lane lined with a rail fence. Dread gathered inside him. He hated the depredations of Indian attacks. He rose in the stirrups, and could see the house had been burned. What about the family? He felt the results would be predictable—butchered bodies.

Apaches could be vicious, especially when after revenge. He could see an undressed form strung over the fence. He waved for Della to stay back.

"Oh, no," she said, steadying the chestnut and making him stay beside him.

"Stay back," he said to her, but she kept her horse crowded close to his.

The body of a boy in his teens, stripped naked and badly mutilated, lay sprawled across the rail fence as if he had been crucified. The sight of his stark white skin and the bloody wounds made a grisly sight.

"Oh, Slocum, she had three girls too."

He shook his head, pushing on. He tried to make sure nothing moved. One hand rode on his gun butt, the other holding down the snorting gray under him. It was obviously upset by the odors of the smoldering fire and death.

"Slocum, there's more—"

"Yes, I see them, Della. The Apaches came after the scouts were here to warn her, I'd say."

"She had the wagon ready to leave, didn't she?" Della asked in a wavering voice.

"Looks that way." He drove the gray up to examine the rig. A child lay facedown under it, and he saw the woman's body in the wagon bed. He quickly turned and blocked Della's view.

"You don't need to look."

"Her?"

"Yes."

"What can we do?"

"Nothing. We'd best push south to Alma. Loco's gone mad."

"The bodies?" Her blanched face was close to tears.

"We'll come back with help and bury them later." He studied the timber beyond the hay meadows, but saw nothing out of the ordinary. It was time to get their untried horses going. The two of them couldn't expect to hold out by themselves. He made her start for the road. One last look at the carnage, and he sent the gray after her.

By mid-afternoon clouds had begun to gather. Slocum and Della crossed a vast open space, and he felt the skin on his neck tingling. Any minute a band of bucks could swoop out of one the islands of pines on the knolls. He made their weary colts trot some more.

"Beckman's store is ahead," she said.

"We may skirt by it," he said, thinking that a store might draw the renegades.

"What if they need help?"

"Who's there?"

"A jack Mormon named Beckman, sells some beer and whiskey. Keeps a few store things. He has an Apache wife."

"We can stop by."

He stopped short of the place and viewed it at a distance for any sign of the Apaches. The corrals and buildings looked normal. No one was in sight. No smoke either, but he still felt edgy. The day was about gone and they were still a long way from Alma. Somewhere ahead, they'd need to camp for the night and he didn't relish the idea, in a strange land he wasn't familiar with and with no idea where the Apaches were.

They rode in closer and could see the cabin and corrals. He searched hard. No smoke came out of the chimney. There was bound to be a cooking fire if anyone was there. Perhaps they'd already left. No doubt the scouts had warned them too. Slocum drew his Colt and pushed in closer to look some more. Their two horses showed road weariness. His gray snorted and dropped his head repeatedly. They sure couldn't outrun any renegades if that was their only option.

"Stay back," he said, and whirled at the click of a gun being cocked. She had her double-barrel ready.

"I'm sticking to you like tar. I can shoot this thing."

He hoped she didn't have to. The corral was open and empty. Warily, he dismounted and gun in hand, walked to the door.

He knocked twice, then pulled the drawstring and stood back when the creaking hinges let the door open. A body was sprawled on the floor. With caution he entered, and could see the person had been shot. It was the one called Josh.

"Who is it?" she asked, keeping guard with the shotgun and blocking the doorway.

"One of those three came by your place. The older one called Josh. Took a bullet. I guess they tried to patch him up."

"What do you think?"

"Beckman and them have left here, I would say." He looked

around. There were signs of hasty departure, things strewn about, not ransacked, but abandoned.

"What do we do next?"

"Find a place to camp for the night. I don't want to stay here."

"There's some Indian ruins in a canyon not too far from here. Apaches won't go there. Place of the dead, they call it."

"Sounds like my kind of place," he said, and headed for the door.

"Sort of strange. Why was Josh killed here? They must have had trouble." She uncocked the scattergun.

"They had a guide too."

"I'm thinking about that. I like him. I wouldn't miss those fellas as much as I'd miss Charlie Two Horse. He does me lots of favors."

"Well, they had a wagon and took it south," he said, examining the tracks in the damp soil. Strange thing, but from the prints they didn't have any other horse, only the team. If the three others had been there with Beckman and left Josh—they must be riding with Beckman in his wagon.

Strange.

"We better hurry—those storms are headed this way," she said, and pointed out the building thunderheads he could see through the boughs.

He shook out the slickers and handed her one. Despite the push, he soon realized they would never beat the storm. The sky crackled, and they hurried under giant ponderosas up a side canyon. He kept his eye peeled for any sign of Apaches, hoping he and Della could find this place she led them to before the rain started. Soon they were deluged by the downpour, with blinding lightning and cannon-fire thunder. He gave a shiver and pushed the tired gray after her.

She led them up a steep rock face. Sheets of water cascaded off, and their horses' footing was doubtful until at last they came under a great overhang. The runoff formed a curtain in front of the hollow under the bluff.

"Not a bad place," she said over the peel of thunder.

"Good place." He removed his sodden Stetson and looked around at the ruins. Several of the room walls remained, and it was dry under the rim. It made a secure campsite.

"What about the horses?" she asked.

"I have some corn we can feed them. They're too tired to graze anyway with the storm and all."

She clapped the chestnut on his wet slick neck. "They did good for such green colts."

"They did very good. I figure we must be a third of the way to Alma?"

"Close to that. Maybe we can make the Darby Ranch tomorrow. He usually has several cowboys. And I'm certain we can borrow fresh horses from him anyway."

"Sounds good. These colts won't have much left in them after another day's ride." With numb, water-wrinkled fingers, he undid the latigos. Once he had their horses unsaddled, he planned to see about some firewood. He flinched as thunder boomed close by, and she shared a frown with him from where she worked to undo her cinch.

He removed his saddle and then slipped under the gray's head and took hers off. Both horses were hitched to the makeshift rack an earlier visitor had installed. He stretched his tight back muscles and raised his hands over his head.

"Better go find some fuel," he said.

"I could go help you."

"No, you stay dry and inside. Feed those horses some of that grain. I'll be right back."

The rain drilled him when he left the protection of the overhang. He kept an eye peeled in the downpour, and soon had an armload of sticks and broken limbs. She smiled with relief at the sight of his return.

With some effort, they finally built a small fire and she cooked coffee. Settled in, he sat on top of a bedroll with his back to a wall. He felt drowsy and dozed some sitting up. He awoke with a start and rubbed his face with his hands. Sleep had not been a major concern for them up till now. The previous night he had been restless, and gotten up several times to check on things. Maybe in this forbidden place he could rest easier.

"Coffee?" she asked.

"Sounds great. Darby's ranch is about how far from here?"

"It's perhaps twenty miles."

He thought about that. That would be plenty of distance for the young horses. Hip-shot and spent, they stood asleep a few yards from him. They'd barely eaten the corn she'd fed them. He wanted to believe Darby had horses to lend them, or perhaps there would be some fortification there if he had cowboys and others armed.

"Kind of strange about that one fella being shot, wasn't it?" she said. "And they never buried him either."

"My guess is they didn't have time and they all left in the wagon. That might mean the Apaches got their horses too. No telling if any of the rest of them survived, for that matter."

She sat on her legs and studied her cup. "You know, I always thought it would have been easier to have died than be taken a captive. You have to live with the scars of that for the rest of your life."

"You feel like telling me about it?" he asked her, never having heard her story.

"We were going west," she said. "Three wagons, a herd of cattle, not a big one, but it was ours. My oldest sister, Fay, and her husband, Buck, had one wagon. Our neighbors from Palo Pinto County, Hap Kenyon and his wife, Zola, my two younger sisters—guess they all died that day. Mom and Dad too—it was like some crazy, earsplitting hell. Shooting and screaming, those Apaches swooped down on us. I never saw the likes. I really didn't know what to do. I loaded rifles for Buck until they shot him, then loaded them for Fay. Two bucks drug me off and—they—" She quit talking. The water spilling off the rimrock sounded loud crashing on the rocks below. "They took turns raping me," she finally said.

"I wanted to die. I felt so disgustingly soiled. I'd lost my virginity. My honor. After that, those two jerked me up and forced me on a horse bareback. They left the fight and took me with them. Some of my family was still fighting them. I can remember they were still shooting.

"Those two were young. Hardly more than my own age, and they must have thought the older warriors would take me away from them. They led the horse I was on and he didn't want to lead. Had his neck stretched all the time. That night they gambled to see who did it to me first. I was so numb, I didn't know anything. Where I was. I didn't eat what they offered me. They were faceless to me. They hardly knew much more than I did about how to do it, and that I had learned from watching animals. I could have had worse luck, if I'd been captured by some big-endowed buck and been ripped apart. These weren't that, but I didn't know. They felt very big to me.

"But they soon wore out and every time they tried to rape me, they couldn't do it. That made them savage toward me. One beat me with a switch like it was my fault. Then I lost track of time. Days and nights all ran together. They were taking me up to Slatter's place to trade me off, but I didn't know their plans or what they talked about. When I saw he was a white man I wanted to die.

"That they acted ruined bothered me too, but I was so sore I never wanted to do it again. Why they couldn't get it hard again, I never knew. I guess they wore it out, so after the first day, one of them would drag me off through the greasewood and then wallow on top of me, so the other one would think he'd got it stuck into me.

"So they traded me to Slatter. They left me there for some rifles, blankets, and pots. They could use them. Neither one could use me. I wanted to die. I said that, but I didn't. After they left, Slatter said, 'Girl, get your head up. Ain't no shame what you did. They're the ones should be ashamed.'

"I lived under his roof for six months. I learned how to raise my head up, and one morning he said, 'You must be healed, girl. You've got your head up all the time now. Here's what we can do. I can take you down to the Southern Pacific Railroad and put you on the train and send you back to your people, or if you don't want to do that we'll get married. What will it be?'

" 'Why's that?' I asked him.

" 'You're too damn pretty to look at and not have,' he answered.

" 'Have?' I asked, dumb as can be.

" 'Yeah, have. Well, what will it be?'

" 'Guess I want to be haved,' I said. Then I ran over and kissed him."

"I knew you and him were close," Slocum said.

"He was good to me. Taught me how to live again. Told me the day he died to find me another man."

"So?"

"I wanted you—still do."

"You know my problems. Things won't change in my life." He shook his head; the situation made his stomach upset.

"Can't you hire lawyers?"

"I've got maybe a dollar and a half in my pockets, and that rich man owns the judge and jury Fort Scott."

"Nothing you can do about it?" She looked up at him.

"His son is dead. He expects revenge and can afford it. Pays those two Abbott brothers to hound me."

"Can't you stop them?"

"He'd only hire some more and they might be tougher."

"Hmm, I never considered that. I see. Slocum, do you want food or—me?" She twisted and snaked her arms around his neck and poised her mouth inches from his.

Who needed food? He took her in his arms and closed his eyes when her pillowy lips met his. Dry and secure in this ancient place, he savored the fire of her body. He could always eat.

12

They left the ruins before sunup. He wanted an early start.
Without starting a fire or coffee, they chewed on some of her
elk jerky in the saddle and rode under the dripping ponderosas
to the road. They reached it in the first peach light of dawn,
and set out in a long trot for Darby's. Slocum intended to be
there by evening if the animals held out.

Several of the Mormon ranches they passed were empty.
Families had fled in haste, even left their clothes hanging on
the lines. Chickens wandered about looking for scratch, and a
cow plaintively bawled that she needed milking.

In mid-morning, they caught up with a woman and three
young children in a wagon. Her sleeves rolled up, she held a
whip in one hand and the lines in the other. From the look on
her blanched face, she might have seen the devil herself. Her
lathered horses were close to being beyond going.

"Better rein them up and rest them," Slocum said, riding
alongside her.

She gave him a spite-filled look and pulled the horses up.
He dismounted and loosened his cinch. Della did the same.

"You seen any of them bloody savages?" the woman asked,
wiping her sweaty brow on her upper sleeve.

"No," Della said while he checked the horses.

"These animals are about done for," he said, looking them
over with a critical eye.

"Yeah, well, if my cowardly husband hadn't left us up there

87

alone and come got us, instead of sending word—"

"He sent word?" Della squinted her eyes at the woman.

"Yeah, he sure did. Sent it with some bucks. Said for me to come at once to Alma. Him and his new wife are down there where they aren't worried a bit about the bloody Indians."

"If you don't drive the horses slower and stop and rest them, they won't make it much further," Slocum said. Both horses looked close to collapse, and the right one wanted to lie down. They were making small noises in their throats, soaked in sweat, which dripped off every hair, and in poor condition too. They were in much worse shape than the colts he and Della rode, and he figured they were still over a dozen miles from Darby's ranch.

"Can you think of anyone who has any horses between here and Darby's that you could borrow?" he asked.

The woman shook her head. She was skinny, in her twenties, with a very little figure. "Well, we can't sit here all day," she said, warily looking around.

"You're probably right."

"If the Patersons haven't left, we could ride with them," she offered.

"How far up the way are they?" he asked.

"Couple of miles," she said.

She drew his sympathy, but there was no way her animals would go much farther. Determined, she gathered the reins to drive on. With a cluck and pop of her whip she moved out, leaving both him and Della standing in the road beside their horses.

"She's desperate," Della said.

"She doesn't have a great hand to play either. And I can't say her man's real brave sending word by scouts either." Slocum shook his head.

"He may be more afraid of her tongue and whip than the Apaches. What will we do?" Della stepped back for Slocum to pull her cinch tight.

"Go on ahead and look for help for her. Those horses won't last two hours. We'll check Paterson's first, and then ride on to Darby's and come back for her. It's all we can do."

"What if—"

"It's all I can think to do is ride for help."

"Yes."

They mounted up and set their ponies in a trot. They passed her on the next hill, where she was flailing the team to little avail. He promised her help, and they hurried on.

In a short while, they found the Paterson place near the road. Three large boys in their teens armed with rifles came out at their approach.

"Anyone else here?" Slocum asked.

"No, Mother and the small ones went to Alma yesterday," the middle one said. They were big strapping boys in overalls with no shirts, and looked very anxious.

"You seen any of sign of those Apaches?" the oldest asked.

"Only when they stole our horses a few nights ago," Slocum said. "But there is a woman and little children with tired horses coming. You have a team she can borrow?"

The boys shook their heads. "They ran off our stock too."

"Is it Cindy—I mean, Mrs. Devon?" the eldest boy asked.

"She never told us her name," Della said. "You know her?"

"Could be she's our neighbor."

Slocum was beside himself. With only two horses to ride, how could he go back and get them? Time was precious. There was no telling where the Apaches were.

"Then we need to go back and get her," Slocum said. "If you don't have a team, then she needs to stay here with you boys. On the road, she'll sure get attacked if those Indians find her."

"What should we do?" the oldest one asked.

"Have you got anything to ride?"

"A burro and a broodmare."

"Get them. I am going back and get her and the kids. Della, stay here. I'll need your horse." The two youngest boys set out at a run to get their animals.

"But—" she started to protest. Then instead, she dismounted and gave him the reins.

"Be careful," she said under her breath. He nodded.

"Mister," the oldest boy said, "I'll go with you. I can walk and lead one of them if need be."

"Slocum's my name, fellas. This is Della."

"Webb's my name, the short one's Tee, and the middle one's Howard. Pleased to meet you, ma'am."

The pair returned with a very big-bellied mare and a gray burro. Slocum caught the lead on the burro and Webb took the mare. He mounted Della's chestnut without a stirrup. They left with Della telling them to be careful.

The juniper thinned out in this lower country, with mesquite, Spanish daggers, and century plants to go with the prickly-pear beds. The air heated up more than in the mountains. They pushed the horses until Slocum saw what he'd expected. One of the wagon horses was down, the right one, and the other stood hangdog in the harness.

The woman stood up the wagon box and used her arm to block out the sun to see the approaching riders.

"Oh, Webb, it's you," she said, and jerked down her dress top and straightened the waist.

"Hi, Cindy. I mean, Mrs. Devon."

"Get what you can and bundle it up," Slocum said, looking around and feeling that they must hurry. "We're taking you to their ranch. They have no team."

"Worthless husband of mine sent word by them Indians for me to get down to Alma," she muttered to Webb when he helped her down.

"Really?" Webb said, taking the children down.

"What am I going to ride?" a small boy asked.

"How about this burro," Slocum said. There was something familiar between Webb and the woman. It was no business of his, but he also knew many neglected Mormon women found substitutes for absent husbands with other wives. It was more than a coincidence too that Webb had been so anxious to come help him.

Slocum put the boy on the burro and showed him how to hold the mane in his fist, then put a second boy on behind. Webb brought back some things wrapped in a bedsheet. They put that on the mare with the girl on top.

"Webb, don't you have your pretty red horse we rode?" the girl asked.

He shook his head quickly. "No, the Injuns got it, Darleen."

"You two can ride the chestnut double," Slocum said, and Webb and Mrs. Devon nodded. "Watch him, he's green-broke. But I figure he's better to do that on than this gray. You all go on and I'll catch up."

"What about my other things in the wagon?" Mrs. Devon asked.

"We'll hope they don't want them until you can get back," Slocum said. "Get going."

Hell, you could replace things, but not children's lives. He looked at the pitiful done-in horses and shook his head. He stripped the harness off the exhausted animals. They might recover and manage to wander off to water. They would never be worth anything again.

He caught the gray and mounted up. The gelding shifted under his weight. It wouldn't go much further either. Damn, his luck was all bad.

Slocum decided to stay over at the Paterson ranch. The house was defensible with lots of open ground, and with the boys well armed along with Della and himself, they should be able to hold off a large force. Besides, Apaches were more interested in attacking the defenseless rather than meeting an armed force. Since they had already taken the Paterson horses, he felt better about the situation sitting on the porch, listening to the night insects with the Spencer across his lap.

"What next, Boss?" Della asked, serving him a cup of coffee.

He was grateful and nodded to her. He knew the Mormons didn't drink coffee, but she had brought a sack of it from her place.

"I hate to leave everyone here, but I plan to ride to Darby's in the morning and borrow a team," Slocum said.

"I'm going too."

"I'd sure wish you would stay here. Those horses of ours couldn't outrun a short-legged rat."

"Slocum."

"All right. We'll go to Darby's in the morning."

"Thanks," she said softly.

"Finally got those kids asleep," Mrs. Devon said, coming out on the porch. "Cooler out here, ain't it?"

"Yes," Della said.

"Guess I'll be fine staying here until this is over. No need in worrying you two about me and them kids. Webb—that's the oldest one here—he said we could stay until they got Loco. Them boys all got rifles. I don't figure them Apaches will bother us here."

"I'll go borrow a team from Darby if he has one," Slocum said.

"No need. Besides, being as mad as I am at that man of mine—why, I might do something I'd regretted when I got there. No, it's better we stay here and that way me and the kids ain't no worry to you two."

"Whatever you think, Mrs. Devon."

"Cindy, Mr. Slocum, and don't think I ain't beholding to you and her for saving me and them kids. I was sure in a pickle today and really beside myself when you two came along."

Somewhere west of the house, a red wolf howled at the night wind. Slocum listened to another yip. They sounded real enough. He and the boys were taking turns standing guard. He'd taken the first shift.

Webb came out later after Slocum sent Della to bed on the floor inside. The youth—Slocum guessed him to be near eighteen—squatted down beside him on the dark porch.

"Will they come at night?"

"No. If they come at all it will be close to dawn."

"They killed all our dogs," Webb said. "Did that the night they took the horses and mules. Wish we still had Lady. She was a collie—she'd growl if she ever smelled one."

"Listen close. They make quail sounds and hoot like owls. Hard to tell them apart, but if you pay close attention you can tell the difference. You hear that wolf a while ago?"

"Yes. He sounded real," Webb said.

"Did to me too. I'm getting some sleep, but tell whoever is on guard don't be afraid to wake us up if anything, I mean anything, bothers them."

"I will, Slocum. Glad you're here. Dad wants this place

saved and left us in charge. I sure don't want to disappoint him."

"You won't."

Slocum found Della by the starlight flooding into the house. He lay down on the bedroll beside her. She was sound asleep. With his hands folded under his head, he could make out the beaded ceiling boards. Half awake, he watched Cindy get up and slip outside.

"—Been a-missing you, Webb," she said in a hushed voice.

"Me too. Father's had us working hard lately. But I was coming up by there Saturday and see you."

"I kinda figured you would."

"I heard you tell Slocum you were staying here with us."

"Ain't that what you said I could do?"

"Oh, yes, but—"

"But what, Webb?"

Slocum couldn't hear the next part. They whispered. He rolled over and tried to catch some sleep. Wasn't any concern of his, what she and Webb did, anyway. As long as those boys kept a guard, that was all that concerned him.

Before dawn, he awoke, uncertain how long he had been asleep. He arose, picked up his hat and the Spencer, then tiptoed out on the front porch. The boy in the chair was asleep. Damn, the most important time of day too. Light-footed, he stepped off the porch and studied the small slip of purple light on the saw edges of the range to the east. It would soon be light enough to see. He took his time, listened, then worked around the corral and the sheds. Not finding anything suspicious, he drained his bladder. In the cool air, he worked around back to the house, and satisfied there were no Apaches, took a seat on the porch.

He found a small cigar, and struck a match that awoke the sleeping boy with a start.

"Huh?"

"Shush," Slocum said, and drew on it.

"I ain't been asleep long," the boy protested.

"If I'd been an Apache you'd of been dead."

"Guess I better stay awake after this."

Slocum nodded and blew out the smoke. "You better. They won't give you a second chance."

"You reckon they're out there?"

"They are where you least expect them to be."

"Guess so. They killed our dogs that night and stole all the horses and mules and never woke us up."

"Webb told me that's what happened."

"You fought them before?"

"I was a scout for the army."

"Man, I'll be glad when this is over."

"So will lots of folks. So will lots of them."

"Don't tell Webb I went to sleep? You know how big brothers are."

"Okay." Slocum wanted to tell him don't ever do it again, but he saved his lecture. Maybe the boy had learned the importance of staying on his guard.

After breakfast, Slocum saddled their horses. He noticed the black horse from her team had, sometime in the night, wandered into the larger open corral with the watering tank. He stood hip-shot, gaunt, and head down. The dried salt on his long coat made him look almost dappled.

"We're going to be extra careful, Slocum," Webb promised. He came down as Slocum was finishing saddling and ready to lead the horses up to the house to get Della.

"Remember, they will come at the worst time. Dawn with the sun in your eyes would be a good time to attack."

"We'll be ready, and thanks for not saying anything."

"Saying anything?"

"I guess you figured from the kids' talk and all. I've been—well, seeing Cindy."

"Wasn't none of my business."

"I know, but her husband don't treat her right. I'm going to take her away from him when this is all over."

"Good luck, Webb."

"I appreciate your advice on when they'll attack and I'll heed it."

"Good." Slocum watched Della come out of the house. He hoped the next part of their journey went smoother. Strange the army wasn't there. With the size of the force they had in

Arizona, he'd expected they would have been swarming the country by this time. But word traveled slow. Still, those scouts were out warning everyone.

He handed Della the reins, shook Webb's and the other boys' hands, and nodded to Mrs. Devon and the children hanging around her skirt. He hoped he and Della were doing the right thing leaving them behind. Alma would be more secure and should have supplies—extra mouths to feed would only deplete the Patersons' supplies sooner.

He and Della left the ranch at a trot. Neither of them had much to say and faced the next part of their journey in silence. Slocum kept his eyes on the brown grassland studded with century plants and Spanish dagger for any signs of the hostiles. In a wide-sweeping valley perhaps forty miles across, with Mogollons in the east and the San Franciscos in the west, they went down the more well-defined wagon tracks that followed the drainage southward.

Buzzards circled ahead. Unable to see the reason for them, he undid the thong on his Colt. The wind scattered pieces of white paper. Slocum dismounted and caught one. It was a letter. He dropped it and shook his head.

"They must have gotten Sam Walters," she said, and checked her horse. "He's a black man hauls the mail up here."

Ahead, they discovered the overturned buckboard and even more letters scattered across the hillside. Their approach sent vultures into flight. The black's naked body lay facedown pincushioned with arrows, and made a grim scene.

"Oh, poor Sam," she said, and shook her head in disappointment.

"Nothing we can do here," he said, with a wave for her to go on.

Darby's large house and red barn were impressive. They reached the valley it nestled in before noontime. A cowboy cradling a Winchester nodded and welcomed them. He even took his hat off for Della.

"The boss is at the house, folks."

"Thanks." They rode up and dismounted.

A tall lanky man with a gray mustache came out of the

house. He introduced himself as Moss Langley, took his hat off for Della, and shook Slocum's hand.

"What can I do for you two?" Langley asked.

"We're headed for Alma and the Apaches took our horses, except for the two colts we're riding, and we wondered if we could borrow a couple. Mrs. Hughes has a ranch up in the high country."

"Oh, yes, I know about Mrs. Hughes' ranch. I'd loan them if I could, but those red-skinned rascals got our remuda too. Guess we'll all be walking soon."

"How did they do that?" Slocum asked as they took the seats the man showed to them on the porch.

"We were working cattle over by the Friscos and they swept down, took the whole string. We tried to chase them down, but all we found were their worn-out ponies, dead tired and not worth spit—excuse my language, ma'am."

"You're excused, Mr. Langley."

"Moss is my given name. They call me Cap mostly."

"Cap it will be."

"No sign of the army?" Slocum asked.

"They came through here and went west to the Friscos, but they were riding sorrier horses than the Apaches abandoned." Cap shook his head. "Them Injuns do much damage up your way?"

"They murdered one family up on the mountain. We helped a Mrs. Devon and her children get to the Paterson place. Her team gave out. The Apaches stole the most of Paterson's horses too. He left his boys to guard the place and she's staying with them."

"They murdered the mail carrier," Della said. "Poor Sam Walters."

"I told Sam to wait until dark to try and go on. He said the mail had to get up there."

"It's scattered all over. We didn't stop to pick it up."

"No, the less time you spend out there the safer your lives are. You two are welcome to stay here. There's eight of us. Colonel Darby is gone back East right now, but he would extend the same hospitality to you two."

"We'll sure spend the night," Slocum said, and nodded to

Della. She agreed. "Those colts should be rested enough to get us to Alma."

"Stay as long as you want. Make yourself at home. You may take the guests rooms at the head of the stairs. I have some bookkeeping to do if you will excuse me." Cap tipped his hat to her and rose. "Oh, if you can think of anyone with a good bunch of ranch horses for sale, I'm in the market for some."

"So are several more folks," Slocum said, and rose to his feet.

Cap went off into the house, and they sat in the high-back chairs on the porch. The afternoon breeze swept away a lot of the heat. They could view the purple Mogollon Mountains and the grassy hills that rolled off toward them.

"Pretty place here, isn't it?" she said.

"Yes, but I wouldn't swap it for yours."

"No, I like mine."

"It's a damn sight cooler too."

"Yes."

Slocum put their horses in the corral, and a couple of the ranch hands visited with him about the Apaches. They brought him oats for the two colts, and dismissed his offer to pay them.

"Major can afford oats," the older one said. "Besides, he's got a bin full of them oats and we've just got the horses we were riding. Man, I sure dread going back up there after them cattle. Had to let them go, didn't have enough horses to ever drive them down. Must of had eight hundred head gathered."

"Loco's upsetting lots of things," Slocum agreed, and thanked them before going back to the porch.

"Time to wash up," Della said. "The cook told me to warn you so we could wash before he rings the bell and all the hands come."

They washed, and the older man came out and rang the bell.

"Right in there, missy. Fill your plate as many times as you like. We ain't got nothing to do around here but eat, so I'm supposed to fill them until their bellies bloat."

"Good idea," she said, and they filed in to fix their plates off the assortment spread on the first table. No one would starve at the Darby Ranch, Slocum quickly decided. There was roast beef sliced in great slabs, potatoes mashed and roasted, green beans, brown beans, boiled greens, a stack of oven-brown biscuits, fresh butter, and a large pan of peach cobbler. Those cowboys might well bloat.

They all smiled and tried to keep from looking at Della, who no doubt looked better than even Cookie's food, Slocum decided. He savored the meal and enjoyed each bite.

"Been lots of folks going by here in wagons and such," Cap said. "They must have a crowd down there at Alma or they've went on down to Silver City."

"I imagine there's plenty already there."

"How many braves did you think Loco had when they took your horses?" Della asked.

Cap motioned to the youngest one. "Bart, how many came after you when they took the horses?"

The shiny-faced boy of perhaps sixteen looked a little embarrassed. "I figured a hundred or more. They were shooting and whooping like crazy."

"He was the wrangler with the remuda when they struck."

"Morning?" Slocum asked.

"No, late afternoon," Cap said. "They knew the horses we rode all day were worn out from gathering cattle, and knew we couldn't chase them far on those ponies. They were right too."

"They might not have been over fifty, but I heard them clear over the hill at the chuck wagon and came running with my old scattergun," Cookie said, refilling coffee cups around the table from a large granite pot.

"They were so fast, they were gone like that." The cowboy snapped his fingers. "Like lightning, bang, and they were gone."

"You had raids before?" Slocum asked.

"Oh, we've had a small party or two slaughter a steer that we knew about," Cap said, holding his coffee cup in both hands. "I kinda figured that was just paying them for the range. They were here first and they needed to eat. But this horse raid was something else."

"Major, he'll be hopping mad when he gets back," one of the other cowboys said.

"He'd been here he couldn't have stopped them either," Cap said in reply.

"He'll still be mad."

"Mad won't hardly count," Cookie began. "Going to be some sad funerals in this country. Cap said you seen old Sam was killed and that Morman family. Be some more good folks bite the dust before they stop this Loco."

"I'd bet good money he gets off scot-free and runs right back down in Mexico," a cowboy offered.

"Army can chase him down there."

"Yeah, but finding him? Be harder than looking for a needle in a haystack."

Slocum knew what the men talked about. Those labyrinths of canyons in the Sierra Madre Mountains left many men lost for days.

"I didn't know better, I'd say they had a supplier too," Cap said.

"What does that mean?" Slocum asked.

"I think someone's selling them arms and making a lot of money off of it. Them Apaches aren't fools. They know where the gold is at in these mountains. Years ago they thought it was bad luck to dig it, but I'd bet a month's wages they don't now. And besides, they steal lots of money off their victims."

"Be pretty messy blood money," Slocum said, reminded of the sight of the murdered family.

"Why, there's men would do anything for a dollar in this world."

Slocum agreed with a nod.

After lunch he and Della retired to the porch.

"We may not find horses at Alma," she said, concerned.

"Oh, they aren't that scarce. We can go down to Silver City if there aren't any there. There are lots of horses left in the world. The Apaches haven't stolen them all."

"Cap believes that about someone selling the Apaches guns, doesn't he?"

"He may know the truth."

"That would be so bad. All these people killed like poor old Sam and that Mormon family."

Slocum studied a hawk riding the updraft, and agreed with

a nod. If there were such lowlifes, they needed to be taught a lesson. He rose. The military was coming in. He could see the company guidon and flag fluttering. Ahead, out in front with a big grin on his face, was the scout Tom Horn.

Cap came out. "See those horses they're riding? Crow bait." He shook his head in disgust.

"Slocum!" Horn shouted, and bounded off his horse. Dressed in buckskin, he came racing over and bear-hugged Slocum. "Man, you are a sight for sore eyes!"

"Good to see you, Tom. This is Della Hughes."

"Why, lordy me, ma'am. You've got to pardon my poor manners. I was so excited to see old Slocum here, I overlooked you and, man, I must have been plumb blind to do that."

"Nice to meet you, Mr. Horn."

"Lordy, ma'am, my name's Tom, and anyone calls me mister is sure talking to the wrong fellar." He swept off his hat and made a bow. "You sure are pretty as a speckled pup if you don't mind me saying so, ma'am."

"Della."

"Yes, ma'am, Della. Well, howdy, Cap. We ain't found your horses yet either."

"I'd imagine they'll all be run in the ground when you do."

"We got us a problem, all right. That new supply of remounts they promised us ain't made it yet either."

"I can see," Slocum said, watching the troops dismount. The exhausted horses looked completely worn out. Why, Loco could ride burros and outrun them. He had the good ranch horses and there was no doubt his raiding would continue unless he ran smack into the army. But Loco was no fool. The chances of him doing that were slim.

Slocum listened to Horn go on talking to Della. His old scouting partner remained the world's biggest flirt. Slocum had serious competition.

13

Slocum and Della prepared to leave Darby's for Alma with the sun peeking over the Mogollons. Tom Horn joined them at the corral.

"You should be safe enough going that way," Horn said. "Not much the army can do about this bunch of renegades but traipse around after them and hope we get lucky. Without remounts, them soldiers might as well be on foot."

"They need Crook brought back here," Slocum said, finished cinching the gray.

"Yeah, or they need to hire some civilian packers with mules for supplies, buy some tough mustangs, and hire thirty Apache scouts to ride them. I would guarantee that a good officer with a force like that could rout Loco and the others in a few days."

"Will the army do that?" Slocum asked as Della swung into the saddle on her chestnut.

"Al Sieber has his way, they will. We won't ever catch these bucks with that bunch of crow baits those troopers are riding. Besides, it takes an Apache to catch one."

"It all pays the same, I guess. Cap Moss said something I've wondered about ever since. He thinks someone is selling those Apaches arms and ammo for gold and cash."

"That wouldn't surprise me one damn bit. Tucson is crawling alive with folks making money every day selling supplies and beef to the army and the Indian agencies. Why, they'd sell their grandmother for a nickel."

"Maybe those sorry horses are on purpose," Slocum said under his breath. "You catch the Indians and the army might need less soldiers, and that would mean less business."

Horn jerked off his weathered cowboy hat and scratched his thatch of hair. "Aw, damn, you don't figure so, do you?"

"More I think on it, the more I wonder."

"Hey, you could be right." Horn slapped his hat on and grinned big for Della. "Ma'am, I sure will be by to see you next time I'm up on top near your place. Old Slocum here has kept you a plumb secret. Been a pleasure to meet you."

"I'd be pleased for you to come by," she said. "Don't let those Apaches get you."

"No way, ma'am. I don't aim for that to happen. See you, hoss."

"Good luck, Horn," Slocum said, and booted the gray out of the corral. He waved to Cap on the porch. Earlier he'd thanked the foreman for his hospitality.

The sun's orange was rising over the Mogollons when they struck the road south. Slocum mulled over the notion of someone supplying the hostiles—on purpose. Pretty gruesome to think about, all those lives lost so someone could make a profit off the Indian uprisings. Be a mean sumbitch that would do that sort of thing.

"Your friend Tom Horn is a nice fellow," Della said, breaking into his thoughts as they rode.

"He'll probably come by and see you now you've invited him."

"He said he would. But he's another drifter like you." She wrinkled her nose at him.

"Yes, he is."

"Oh, well, a drifting man is better than no man at all."

They both laughed and set their horses into a trot.

It was past noon when they reached Alma. With the many parked wagons and their teams close by grazing, it looked like a large center of population. Slocum could see that the Apache threat had brought lots of settlers and their families to this place on the small creek for protection.

"Seen any Apaches?" a man toting a rifle asked them.

"No sign since we left Darby's place this morning."

"You come by Paterson's?"

"Yes, we did. Two days ago."

"Those boys holding that place?"

"They were doing fine, but the renegades hadn't tried to attack them there yet. On the trail we found where the Apaches killed the postman Sam."

"Hate to hear that. He was a good man. You see that wagon up there? That's the Patersons'. They've been concerned about those boys. You wouldn't mind to stop and tell them, it would make them feel better."

"We couldn't bury poor Sam, but we told the army about him," Della said. "And the Strong family on the Burn Meadow, they were—massacred too."

"Oh, that's bad news. Bad," the man said, and went on his way.

Slocum reined up at the Paterson wagon. A thin woman in her forties came with her skirt in hand to meet them.

"Mrs. Paterson?"

"Yes?"

"We were at your ranch two days ago and the boys were fine. Mrs. Devon and her children joined them. Her horses broke down, so she's there too."

"Oh, my, thank you so much. That's good news about my boys. Thanks. Carl's convinced they can hold the place. I've sure been worried about them."

"Mister, mister." A man came running, dressed in a suit and tie. "My wife is supposed to be coming. She should be here. You didn't see her on the road?"

"Your name Devon?" Slocum asked.

He held his hand up against the sun. "Yes, you know about her?"

"She and the children are fine, but the horses broke down and she's at Paterson's place."

"Horses broke down? Oh. I wondered why she hadn't made it here."

Slocum nodded to Della to ride on. He had to bite his tongue. If that coward had been so worried about her, why hadn't he gone to see about her? Slocum suspected that what Webb said about how her husband mistreated the woman was probably true.

"I wonder if we can even find any horses for sale here," Della said as they rode into the community. Many children ran about and played in the warm sun. Rigs were parked all along the road. Wagons, tents and makeshift shelters of blankets and tarps filled the valley. Clothes were hung to dry everywhere, and team horses stood flicking flies with their tails.

"There's a saloon ahead," Slocum said. "I'll go in there and see what I can learn. We may have to go on to Silver City."

"I'll wait in the shade over there." She motioned to a mesquite tree nearby.

"I'm not going to camp in there," he said with a grin.

"Don't worry, take your time."

He stepped off the gray and handed her the reins. She rode off to the shade leading his horse. With a smile, he crossed the porch and pushed in the bat-wing doors. The sour smell of beer and stale cigar smoke filled his nose.

The crude bar was mounted on kegs and the man behind it looked at Slocum with one eye closed. Obviously smoke from the cigar wedged in the corner of his mouth stung that eye.

"What'll it be?"

"Whiskey and a few answers."

"Whiskey costs two bits, answers are varied."

The man poured a shot glass full, and Slocum dug out the quarter, which reminded him of his poor financial state. He slapped it on the counter.

"Need about a half-dozen good ranch horses," he said.

"Have to go to Silver City. Ain't none up around here for sale."

"So to Silver City." Slocum raised the glass and toasted the man.

"You just come down the road?"

"Yes."

"How far?"

"From up on top."

"You were lucky. Didn't see them red devils?"

"They stole all the ranch horses five days ago."

"Must be eating them. Why, they've stolen more horses than you can count. Want another?" The barkeep poised the bottle for a refill.

"Nope." Slocum held his hands out. "Thanks."

"Yeah, I hate it, but really, this Injun deal ain't bad for business."

"I bet it isn't. See you." Everyone made money off the Indian scare.

Slocum left the bar. That man probably had more business than ever. Strange he had never thought about making profits out of murder and mayhem. If this raid went on much longer, there would be a call for even more soldiers to be sent. He'd bet there wouldn't be any call for better remounts.

Outside, he had to adjust his eyes to the brilliant light. He headed to where Della rested under the small tree. Charlie Two Horse was squatted there.

"What did you learn?" she asked, standing up and brushing off the back side of her leather riding skirt.

"Silver City next stop."

"We may have learned what happened to those men," she said, tightening her cinch. "Talk to Charlie."

"We stopped at Beckman's," Charlie said. "That Josh was going to clean his gun and shot himself. Crazy thing, bang, and he was on the floor. Apaches came by and stole all the saddle horses that night, so Beckman took his wagon and we all came down here. We didn't stop till we got here."

"Where did Randy and Tad go after that?"

"They took the Silver City stage. Beckman and his squaw are camped across the wash."

"What are you going to do?"

"Try to buy me a damn horse and go home—alive." Charlie laughed.

"Randy and Tad are probably in Mexico guarding those gold shipments by now." Slocum shared a smile with the Apache.

"Reckon we will find any horses in Silver City?" Della asked, sounding concerned.

"If we don't, I'll wire Texas and find some," Slocum replied.

"Nice to have friends with connections," she said, and swung her leg over the chestnut's butt. In the saddle she settled down and then smiled at him. "Charlie, you could go with us, but we don't have but these two colts you sold me."

"Getting pretty good broke too. I'll find something to ride. See you," he said, and waved them on their way.

Slocum swung in his saddle and glanced over at her. Her good looks took his breath away at times. Maybe they would travel on forever—he didn't know.

"We going now?" she asked.

"I don't see a reason to stay here."

"Let's ride."

Long past dark, they reached Gustoff's place on the Gila, a stage station and wagon yard under the gnarled cottonwoods in the moonlight. A Mexican guard with a rifle nodded to them from his place on the front porch.

"See any 'Paches?" he asked.

"Not in days," Slocum said as they dropped heavily from their saddles.

"They're still out there—somewhere."

"I don't doubt that. Got any food left in there?" He tried to restore the circulation in his legs and stomped his boots around.

"Plenty food. Mary, she will fix it for you." The guard nodded toward the open door.

Mary, a buxom Mexican woman, came out of the back when they entered the room.

"You want food?" she asked.

"Yes."

"I have some hot. Take a seat anywhere," she said, and went back for it.

The room contained several rough board tables, and he and Della sat opposite each other. A big black-bearded man came in the room.

"You see any Apaches?"

"Not between here and Alma. Actually, we left Darby's this morning," Slocum said.

"You come a fair piece. Been keeping a guard. They tried to steal my horses about ten days ago, but we stopped them in time and they rode off."

"You were lucky," Della said. "They stole all my stock, and even got away with Darby's entire remuda."

"Maybe they have enough horses by now."

"I hope so. It's making horses scarce," she said.

"Yeah, folks need something to ride around here may find they're using shoe leather."

"I'm counting on some horses being for sale at Silver City," Slocum said.

"Usually are." The man nodded to them when Mary brought two plates heaping with food. "I'll let you two eat. There's a small cabin out back if that would suit you."

"Yes, fine," Slocum said.

"Freddie will show you where it is when you are ready. See you in the morning."

"Thanks," Slocum said, his stomach growling at the prospect of the delicious-smelling food the woman delivered to them.

"Silver City tomorrow?" Della asked.

He nodded, and she winked mischievously at him. Might not get much rest again. Oh, well.

14

Two days later, they had taken a room in the San Reyes Hotel in Silver City. The town was abuzz with rumors of Loco and his band. Two companies of soldiers were stationed there to protect the town. Many ranch families from outlying areas had camped around the town, much like at all the other settlements.

Slocum wired T. K. Adams in El Paso about horses, and waited for the man's answer. Adams had connections with many outfits and could probably get horses on the way quicker than any other dealer. Cap Moss at Darby's ranch wanted a hundred head, and Della needed a dozen. So the order was sizeable enough that they should get some attention.

At the sight of a rider in the street, Slocum guided Della into a doorway of a store.

"What's wrong?" she asked softly.

"Don't look now, but my old buddy Charlie Forsyth just showed up here. He still owes me ninety-six dollars," he said under his breath with his back to the street.

"That's the one called in the Abbott brothers on you?" She frowned in disapproval at Forsyth.

"That's the same one. He didn't see me. Wonder what he's up to here." Slocum watched the man stop at the livery and leave his horse, then take his valise and head for the Plaza Hotel. He must have business here. He didn't have that working woman with him that he took the money from in Socorro.

"What are you thinking?" Della asked.

"It shortens my lead a little. Him in town, and if he knew I was here he'd go to wiring for those Abbotts."

"What'll we do?"

"We get that wire back from Adams and we'll know more. Let's go check on it at the telegram office." He herded her along with an eye toward the hotel. He'd bet that Forsyth didn't do any more than put his valise in a room and head for a card game.

They stepped into the small telegraph office, and the man behind the counter nodded.

"Got you an answer."

"Good," Slocum said, and took the message. Satisfied that he could see anyone who came or went out the front door of the hotel, he quickly read it aloud.

"Have horses there in ten days. My man at Fort Griffin is starting out in two days. Has a hundred and fifty good using horses. Several came from the same outfit. Try to sell the rest for me. Cost thirty-five a head there. Any problem, let me know."

"Not cheap, but not bad," she said.

"Can you use them at that price?" he asked.

"Sure. I can use a dozen."

Slocum wrote a message for Adams:

"Darby Ranch north of Silver City wants a hundred. See Cap Moss. Leave a dozen for Della Hughes at Silver City, and will find buyers for the rest. Slocum."

The click of the key signaled an incoming message, and the operator busied himself with it. When he finished, he shook his head.

"Loco and his bunch swept down on San Carlos Agency yesterday, killed ten police, and stole several women."

"They'll be on the move then," Slocum said. That was why no one had heard from them in several days—they were way west. Loco drew the army off to the east, then swept down in the west like some military strategist would do.

"Where will they head next?" she asked.

"Mexico," Slocum said.

"Good, then we can go home."

"What about the horses?" he reminded her.

"You mean we have to stay here until then?"

"If you want those horses you better."

"What will you do?" she asked as they pushed out onto the porch.

"I better make tracks after I collect my money from Forsyth."

"I was afraid of that."

"There he goes now. I missed my guess. He's going in the mercantile."

"Must need something," she said.

"Why don't you go shopping?"

"I could do that. Where will I meet you?" she asked.

"At the hotel. Find out anything you can about what he's up to."

Slocum watched her cross the street between the traffic of rigs and wagons. When she went in the mercantile, he headed for the livery.

"Man just came in, a Mr. Forsyth," he said to the livery hand leaning on a pitchfork.

"Yeah, that's his bay over there,"

"He wants the shoes pulled off him. The last guy shod that horse got them on crooked, and he wants that horse's feet to rest while he's here. He's going to be here several days and he sent me over to tell you. He'll pay you fifty cents a hoof to take them off."

"That isn't any problem, I'll do that right now." The man smiled at the prospect of that sum of money, showing his tobacco-brown teeth.

"Sure thing. I'll tell him you're handling it. What's your name?"

"Riley."

"Good man, Riley, and he'll be by to pay you for doing it too."

"Why, I'll have them off quicker than a lamb can wag her tail."

"Good man," Slocum said, and left the livery. Wondering what Della would learn, he went back to the room and played solitaire on the bed until he heard the door rattle.

She burst in out of breath. "You aren't going to believe what I heard."

Slocum rushed to the door, checked the empty hallway, and then closed the door. "What?"

"They—well, the man who owns the mercantile and Forsyth have ten cases of Winchesters they are going to deliver to Loco at the Gila crossing."

"Which crossing?"

"That was all I heard them say. The Gila crossing. And for a thousand dollars in gold nuggets."

"How did you learn all that?"

"I used the changing room next to the office, and the wall was so thin. This other fella knew Forsyth from somewhere else. They spoke about a man called Yarborough."

"I know him. Tough character. Is he here?" Slocum frowned at the notion that Yarborough was there. He knew the man on sight.

"No, but he's got a pack string. They are taking the rifles by wagon to meet him."

"So Forsyth is teamed up with this merchant and they're meeting Yarborough, who's going to pack them in for them."

"That's what it sounded like. What're we going to do?"

"You're going to keep your pretty butt right here in the hotel. I am getting word to Tom Horn. Maybe we can stop them."

"You said 'we'?"

"Tom Horn and a handful of good Apache scouts."

"But I thought they didn't have any horses to ride, or any good ones."

"Tom Horn and those Apaches can steal some horses if they have to."

"How will you get him word?"

"I guess you'll have to ride up there and tell him while I track the wagon to wherever Yarborough is at."

"How will they ever find you?"

"Those Apaches scouts of his can find me."

"When do I do this?" she asked, looking very concerned.

"In the morning."

"What if Tom isn't at Darby's anymore?"

"Chances are he'll be there or at Alama guarding the citizens."

"Two days ride?"

"Better make it in one. Rest that pony good when you get there."

"What if he isn't anywhere to be found? Tom Horn?"

"Then you better pray for me. I don't intend to let those butchers have those rifles."

"Slocum?" She frowned at him.

"You find Horn. Tell him that they're meeting at a crossing on the Gila and to meet me with a small force of scouts to stop them."

"But where is the crossing?"

"He'll have to come downstream and find it. Those Apaches of his will find it."

"But I thought you said Loco would go to Mexico."

"That's what Loco wanted them to think. The military has shifted all their forces east by this time and he's headed southeast. Those greedy bastards selling them rifles—wonder how Forsyth got hooked into it."

"He made the arrangements with Yarborough for the mules."

"Sounds like that conniving rascal. That's all right. They aren't going to deliver those arms to Loco's band if I can help it." He went to the window and gazed down at the front of Ludman's Mercantile. Who was Ludman and why was he so fired up to make blood money? Why, if folks knew what he plotted to do, they would never trade with him again.

The shoes were pulled off Forsyth's horse. What else could he do? Next he had to cripple one of the buggy horses, not seriously, but enough to slow them down until Horn could meet up with him.

"You know who that is pulled up to Ludman's in that wagon?" she asked.

"No."

"That's Beckman and his squaw on the wagon seat. Randy and Tad are down there too. They must have found some horses."

"You don't reckon that they are transporting the rifles to

Yarborough?" Slocum didn't relish the prospect. "Things are unfolding faster than I like to think."

"Why don't you go to the commander of those soldiers camped at the edge of town and tell him."

"He won't believe me. Ludman is a very important merchant and a member of the community. Besides, we still don't get Yarborough and he's the toughest one of all."

She kissed him on the side of the face and wrapped her ripe form around him. "Nothing we can do until dark, is there?"

"No, really not." He looked down at her. "If we must, we must."

15

Slocum pried the wooden lid open with an annoying creak. Della held the small candle lamp closer. He could see the reflection from the well-oiled metal gun barrels inside the case. The new repeaters were lined up side by side.

"That doesn't look like mill machinery parts to me," she whispered.

"They were smart enough to change boxes," he said, and pressed the lid back down. Satisfied it looked the same, he tapped in the nails, then blew the candle out. Ten cases of Winchester rifles bound for the Apache renegades. They represented a thousand dollars in gold or cash, and many more innocent lives would be lost for greed.

He followed on her heels and they left the warehouse. No one would even suspect the well-concealed weapons. "Mill Machinery Parts" was stamped on the boxes in big black letters, along with "Brocom Metal Works, Bridgeport, Connecticut."

"What do Randy and Tad have to do with all this?" she whispered in the alley.

"Damned if I know, but they're in on it and so is Yarborough."

"We know they do have rifles. Can't we tell the military and have them handle it?" she asked under her breath.

"I wish it were that simple. We need all of them rounded up and stopped. Forsyth and Yarborough as well as Ludman.

I want every one of them arrested." He cast a glance at the mercantile across the street. If he could only collect his money from Forsyth, then round up all the gunrunners, he would have his cake and eat it. But he'd have to be lucky to do all that, and his luck had been slim of late.

"What're you doing?" she asked from behind him.

"Dreaming how to get my damn money back."

"If he learns you're even in the country, he'll wire those brothers, won't he?"

Slocum nodded. He couldn't jump Forsyth yet. He turned and smiled at her. "Let's get a few hours sleep. You've got lots of miles to ride tomorrow."

"You think that gray can hold out trailing them?" she asked.

"If he can't, I'll find me another one."

"Where?" she asked. They hurried up the boardwalk for the San Reyes Hotel.

"I have been known to borrow a horse."

"The pickings are small around here."

"You just make it to Darby's in one piece and get Tom Horn notified." It was on his mind. The gunrunners would need to leave soon to even meet Loco. If he came from San Carlos—they'd need to meet him in a day, not more than two, with the army on his backtrail even on poor horses.

Slocum opened the hotel's front door for her. She swished inside and he followed.

"Hold it right there, John Slocum."

The words drew cold chills down his spine. It meant either the law or a bounty hunter. He shook his head quickly at Della, warning her not to do anything. Slocum turned and saw the gun barrel aimed at his gut, then the man behind it. He was in his thirties, well dressed—almost dapper.

"Who are you?" Slocum asked.

"Ezra Bertram. Got me a poster here says that you're worth five hundred dollars. Don't try anything fancy."

"Mister, I don't know who you are, but I can tell you out-right they won't pay it."

"Well, now, little lady, you can go about your business," Bertram said with a wave of his pistol barrel. "I'll be taking that hawg leg and the rest of your hardware, Slocum. You and

me got us a date in that jail and we will see the color of the
Fort Scott sheriff's money."

"Save you plenty of time mister—"

The man took his Colt from behind.

"Tell Horn," Slocum said sharply to her.

"Tell Horn what?" Bertram demanded.

She looked white under her tanned face. Chewing on her
lip, she backed away, then fled up the stairs. Bertram shook
his head at her flight.

"Get moving and don't try nothing." Slocum mildly obeyed
the man's directions to march out the front door. As long as
she went for Tom Horn, that was the most important thing. It
was a long way from Silver City to Fort Scott. When the
money didn't come on demand, Bertram would be mad. It had
happened before, no reason to suspect it wouldn't happen this
time—*just so that she went for Horn.* That was the only real
thing that bothered him. His arrest was a mere inconvenience.
He planned to figure a way out of it and soon.

They marched down the street to the Silver City marshal's
office. Bertram spoke to the sleepy jailer, who wearily rose.
Then they took Slocum back to the row of cells and locked
the door. Slocum dropped on the unpadded bunk and removed
his hat. With his sorry luck, they'd mistake him for some
vicious killer and hang him before the week was out.

"Slocum? I'm going to send that wire. Anything you want
to tell him?" Bertram asked from the doorway.

"Yeah, tell him to send the money. You won't get it. They
won't pay it."

"We'll see." And the man was gone.

Bertram was a skilled pro. Slocum had never detected the
man in his time spent in Silver City. Most bounty men were
much more obvious; he could read them like a book. This one
had slipped up in a business suit and made the arrest in the hotel
lobby. Took all kinds to make the world go around. A hundred
rifles were sitting in the warehouse across the street, and by daylight they would be on their way to the hostile Apaches. He was
locked up in this cell unable to do a thing about the matter.
Maybe Horn could stop them; Della had to get him word.

Two or three days and they'd turn him out—no reward, no

one coming to get him. The Silver City marshal would get tired of feeding him. So long as the Abbott brothers didn't get there before they released him. By then Loco would be well on his way to the Sierra Madres with new arms and ammo if no one stopped him.

Slocum slept lightly on the jail bunk. He fretted the night away about Della getting the word to Horn. At dawn, they marched the prisoners out one at a time to the outhouse in back to relieve themselves. The guard carried a shotgun and warned he would use it. The privy sat across the alley behind the jail in an open field, and making a break would be suicidal. Slocum dismissed the idea as too desperate.

"Leave the damn door open," the guard said.

Slocum relieved himself in the stinky crapper and came back outside. He saw a wagon pulling out in the predawn. Was it the rifles?

"Get your ass in there," the guard grumbled, and he obeyed.

Back in his cell, a black prisoner delivered a big cup of liquid that he called coffee and some cold oatmeal. Slocum took it and ignored the complaints of the others down the way. That was the food. Better to eat it and shut up than go hungry. They complainers might not get any more, to teach them a lesson.

"Your name Slocum?" a big man asked, standing at the bars.

"You the law here?"

"Yeah. This Bertram says you're a killer from Kansas."

"Got the wrong man. They won't pay any reward for me. They won't send anyone after me."

"You sound like this has happened before. I gave Bertram twenty-four hours unless I hear something else sooner."

"Anyone can print them posters."

The man nodded. "Been me, I'd gone out and found the printer." He laughed at his own joke as he went down the hall and into the office.

Good. In twenty-four hours he'd be out. Forsyth didn't know he was in there; more than likely he'd ridden out with those rifles. And Yarborough was mixed up in it. That skunk would be in any deal no matter how sorry. Slocum could only wonder if Della made the journey safely and found Horn.

Slocum was half asleep in mid-afternoon when the big man came back.

"Guess you were right. Sorry for the inconvenience, but the Fort Scott sheriff wired me minutes ago that they have the real John Slocum en route to there by train." He unlocked the cell and threw back the door. "Captured him in Durango, Colorado, three weeks ago."

"Must make them happy," Slocum said, and wondered who they had brought in. Never mind. He needed to make tracks.

"Here's your gun. That Bertram was sure sore when I told him."

"I bet he was," Slocum said, and holstered the Colt.

"Oh, yes, here's a letter for you."

Slocum opened it and saw by the writing a woman had written it.

"Gone to tell Horn. Will be back in two days. Della."

"She leave you?" the law asked.

"Yeah, thank God," Slocum said, and reset his hat on his head.

"Most men would be mad."

"I ain't." Slocum headed for the stables. A new problem had arrived. To get his horse out of the stables, he needed to pay the board bill. That required money, and the last time he'd checked, he'd had none. They had been using Della's money.

"I come to get my gray," he said to the boy.

"Yes, sir." The boy jumped up from the worn sofa.

"That lady pay for him when she rode out this morning?"

"I guess she did. Murphy ain't here right now, but if you say she did, I'll take your word."

Slocum looked around. He had to ride before Murphy got back in case she hadn't. He slung his saddle on the gray when the boy brought him up.

"Yeah, some fella was really mad today," the boy said. "Big mixup. They said to take the plates off his horse, only they must have got the wrong horse. His horse was barefoot and he needed to ride on, and Murphy was mad as a hornet."

"Whew, that does sound bad." Slocum gathered the reins, swung in the saddle, and rode out into the sunlight. He halfway expected someone to challenge him, but no one did. He set the fresh horse into a lope and left Silver City, his heart pounding inside his chest. He wondered if they'd gone north or west with the rifles. The Gila lay in both directions. Then he decided that they had to take the road with the wagon to meet Yarborough. He reached down and felt for the Spencer in the scabbard, grateful that it left him some firepower.

Late afternoon, Slocum paused and spoke with two woodcutters. They had seen a man and a squaw in a wagon and three riders headed north around midday. The cutters had their burros heavily loaded with stove wood and acted anxious not to spend the night in the desert. Slocum let them go on and began to memorize tracks as he rode. It soon became apparent that he was following the same prints that had left Beckman's store when Slocum and Della passed by.

If the rifles were in that wagon, then Slocum wasn't far behind them. The length of the day drew down and he cursed his luck. He still had not caught sight of them. The fiery ball of orange set behind the Friscos, and he knew he would be forced to stop for the night. His stomach complained. The oatmeal had been a long time back. Maybe he had some elk jerky in his saddlebags—he could always hope for some anyway.

If he continued on and overran where they turned off, he might never find them before they switched their cargo to pack mules. He dismounted. Damn, it had been hectic enough, being jailed and all. If Della had found Horn, maybe he could intercept them. Oh, well. Slocum found some jerky wrapped in butcher paper in the saddlebags, and began to try to chew on it. Who did they have bound for the Fort Scott jail? Someone would surely recognize it was not Slocum. People always said everyone had a double somewhere in this world. Poor fella was probably kicking and complaining.

Somewhere off in the night a coyote yipped, and another answered him. Slocum unfurled his bedroll and laid it out. Better to sleep some while he had the chance. By daybreak, he needed to be closer to the wagon. He hobbled the gray and let him graze, then curled up and caught some sleep.

By the time the sky pinked over the Mogollons, he was in

the saddle and pushing north. He almost overrode the tracks where they turned west down a dry wash. Pausing to consider his next move, he used his thumb to rub an itch in the whisker stubble on the right side of his mouth. He dismounted in the faint light and studied the prints. Somewhere out in that jackrabbit-infested country, Yarborough was going to meet the wagon with mules. How far in there could they take Beckman's wagon? No telling. He booted the gray, but didn't want him to lope or trot. He might run smack into them. At midmorning he rode up on a high place and used his brass telescope.

His vision was distorted by heat waves, but the telltale rising dust of the wagon and riders looked two miles ahead. He could see the wisps of brown churned up by their hooves and iron rims. Good enough. The dim road must go a ways yet. He went back and mounted the colt. With the telescope back in his saddlebag, he sent the horse trotting westward.

This close to the rig he felt much better. Maybe he could manage to catch all of them together. Better yet, let Horn and the Apache scouts take them in as gunrunners. Be hard to explain why you had a hundred repeaters out here in the desert, except to deliver them to the hostiles.

Several times he rode up on a high point to check on them; the wagon and men moved on. Then he dropped down and rode along at a comfortable jog. If Horn came down the Gila, Slocum might miss them. He hoped not, and booted the gray up the gravel hillside through the cholla and around great patches of prickly pear. Signs showed in places where the javelina grazed on the stickery pads. Carefully, he peered over the rim and couldn't see anyone. They must have stopped. He reined the horse back down into the wash, tied him to a mesquite bush, and removed the Spencer from the scabbard. From here on he would be on foot. He hoped to get close enough to spy on them and perhaps learn when Yarborough would arrive.

He hugged the cover and kept low. A covey of topknotted quail dispersed into the grass ahead of him. Taking a southerly direction, he hoped to skirt around and not be discovered. There were enough people in this deal. Randy and Tad for guards, Forsyth and the trader Beckman, Beckman's wife, plus whoever Yarborough brought to haul the guns on to the Gila. Here the hills grew taller, Slocum decided, out of breath from hurrying. No doubt the road must have petered out. He stopped and tried to settle his breathing.

Then he started uphill again, and at last gained the next ridge, keeping behind a scrubby juniper. The stiff smell of woodsmoke carried on the wind. Close enough. He better get down and learn all he could about them.

He bellied down under the dusty boughs and studied the camp. Randy was working on his horse's shoe. The kid was talking to him. Forsyth and Beckman must have been on the other side of the wagon—he couldn't see them from his vantage point. With the south wind picked up, he couldn't hear anything over it. Nothing to do but wait. They must be a half day's ride from the Gila, and no telling how far from the crossing.

How would he ever let Horn know where they were at? No way, unless some of his scouts found them. Slocum could hope for lots of things. If Della found Horn and he had taken his scouts out then, they could show up before sundown. Slocum didn't really expect them for another day or more. Horn still had to get permission to go on the scout. The army might not let him—no, Horn could convince them that he was going after gunrunners. Poor Della would be hurrying back to Silver City to try to get him out of jail—and he'd not left her word. But when she learned he wasn't there, then she'd realize he'd gone off after the guns.

He watched Forsyth go over and talk to Randy. From what he could see at the distance, Forsyth must be paying him off. He gave Randy and Tad some money and acted like he was thanking them. They fixed their cinches as if they were going to ride off. Good, that only left Beckman and Forsyth in camp. He didn't figure the squaw would do much.

Randy and Tad rode out. Slocum checked the sky. The sun hung in mid-afternoon. Randy and Tad would never make it back to Silver City by dark, but Forsyth was done with them. Obviously, he didn't want them to know his purpose. He'd probably told them he was delivering mining machinery and needed protection from the Apaches.

Slocum bellied down on the ridge. He was guessing Beckman, through his squaw and dealings with the Apaches, was the contact man with Loco. That merchant Ludman had sent Forsyth along to look out for his interests; Forsyth had connected with Yarborough to supply the mules to deliver the repeaters. It all made a lot of sense from his spot under the juniper. Plenty of middlemen in the deal to pay, but as tight as things were in business, any profit would be a good one.

Wind sounded in his ears and through the branches above him. A noisy raven called out like a sentry as it flew past. "Intruder! Intruder!" The men were out of sight again, and the woman was using a hatchet to chop kindling. Whacks of her ax carried on the turpentine-smelling air. Slocum wondered how long he had to wait.

When the red sun dropped in a notch behind the Franciscos, he rose and went back to his horse. Nothing he could do until morning. The gray made a soft whinny at his approach. He shared the little water left in his canteen. Then he wiped the gray's muzzle and nostrils with his bandanna. They would need to find some water in the morning. There was not much sign of anywhere they'd parked the wagon. Beckman might have a barrel on the side of his rig. It wouldn't last long with three grown-ups and three horses. That might have been why they'd paid off Randy and Tad.

He ate some jerky seated on his bedroll in the twilight, and listened to some red wolves howl in the distance. It was lonely out there with only a few hoot owls and wolves to sing songs at him. He wondered what Della was doing.

At dawn, he heard shooting. Plenty of it. Damn, had Horn stumbled on their camp? No, he could have taken them by surprise with his Apaches. The shooting stopped. Slocum hurriedly rolled up his bedding, tightened the girth, and swung the gray around. Something was wrong at Forsyth's camp. Had Loco found them and taken the rifles?

He reached the top of the ridge, and in the dark shadows of the canyon could see the wagon's outline. Nothing moved, but the tailgate was open. He eased the gray off the hillside,

Colt in his fist. The sun wasn't high enough to see well down the canyon's depth. Then he saw the first body sprawled on its back, an older man, must be Beckman. He rode a wide swath around the camp. Forsyth lay in his frock coat on his side, obviously a gunshot victim from the dark stains on his vest. Where was the woman? He didn't need a hatchet stuck in his head. Cautiously he stepped down and gave the toe of his boot to Forsyth, and the man's limp body rolled away. *Damn, he would never collect his money now!*

This was not the work of Apaches. Whoever shot these two—it had to be Yarborough, for the rifles were gone. Slocum paused, scrubbed his face with his palm, and shook his head. Things got deeper and deeper in this deal. He holstered his Colt and searched Forsyth's pockets. Twelve dollars in total was all he found. Eighty-three dollars short. Still keeping alert, he moved over and searched Beckman's clothing. On him he discovered forty more. The bill was down to forty-five. He straightened and went to the water barrel. He shook it and smiled at the sound—there was a third left.

He watered the grateful gray horse, then found Forsyth's sorrel and watered him. The horse and rig might bring thirty. Satisfied it was all he could do there, he put blankets over the dead men, weighed them down with rocks, and turned the two team horses loose to fend for themselves. With a deep sigh he set out on the trail of the guns.

When he considered what happened, he realized the dead men had never undressed. He wondered if Yarborough had arrived earlier the night before. No telling. The double cross was in effect, and the outlaw planned to keep all the money from the rifles.

Slocum made the gray trot.

16

He could see the distant line of cottonwoods ahead, maybe ten miles further. The Gila had to be close. Slocum had traded horses at midday, and had ridden the sorrel for a few hours. It wasn't the horse that Forsyth had ridden into Silver City. It must be one Ludman had loaned him. Forsyth's actual pony was barefooted and still at the livery when Slocum left there.

Both of the horses were close to spent, and needed a drink as bad as Slocum did. He dropped off into a wash, hoping to find a pocket of water. Yarborough was somewhere ahead of him. From their tracks, the outlaws had not wasted any time moving on since the murders and robbery. Hard to tell how many men were with him from the tracks, but regardless of the number, Slocum still needed to somehow prevent those rifles from falling into the hands of the Apaches.

The descent off the ridge paid off. He rounded a bend and found a spring-fed pool under a bluff. Numerous deer tracks told him the water was palatable. A flock of dusting Sonora doves took wing with a clap at his approach.

He dismounted and fought the horses back. They only needed a small drink if he didn't want them sick; he would be forced to jerk their heads out far short of their fill. No time for a colicky horse. Besides, they could take colic, then twist a gut and die from it. He allowed both of them to drink a few deep draughts and then pulled them away. Water was dripping from their muzzles as he fought them back and eventually led them over and tied them securely to a juniper.

He looked carefully around. Several topknot quails whistled on the hillsides, but nothing moved out of place. He bellied down and drank a little of the cool water. It didn't satisfy his thirst by any means, but he too didn't need to get a bellyache from too much water.

Better he spent some time watering himself and his stock. He could catch up with the gun thieves later. He rose out of the sand and brushed himself off. How much time did he have? If Loco came charging over the mountains, he could be close to the crossing already. Slocum sure didn't want to be there too late, but if the chief had eighty warriors with him as people said, he had no force to stop him unless Horn brought the scouts.

Then an Apache appeared on the rise. Slocum broke and ran for the horses, his boot soles churning up the sand. He jerked the Spencer out—

"Hold your fire!" Horn shouted, and charged up the wash on a stout red roan horse.

Slocum dropped the rifle butt in the sand and shook his head in disbelief. "Speak of the devil and he arrives."

"No, that's Ben-Gone up there. He thought he saw a rider coming off the mountain two hours ago."

"He's got good eyes," Slocum said, shoving the rifle back in the scabbard.

"Where are the rifles?"

"Yarborough and his men killed Beckman and Forsyth this morning before daylight. They took the guns for themselves. How's Della?"

"Captain Eagan gave her a military escort back to Silver City. She thought you were still in jail."

"Got out. How many scouts are with you?"

"Four."

"I thought—"

"Hell, Slocum, if I'd had thirty scouts I'd have already run him down. Four's all I have. My boss, Al Sieber, is threatening to resign if they don't do something different. By damn, I'll quit with him too."

"I savvy. It wouldn't have done any good to have tried to stop them in Silver City. They would have denied the rifles were for the Apaches and we'd have never proved different. I hoped to catch them out here trading, but if Loco has eighty men we don't need to mess with him."

"I would sure like to stop this Yarborough from selling them, though."

"I agree. That's the important part now."

"How far away is he?"

"Ahead of me. I been on his trail all day."

Horn moved out in the wash and waved his arm for the Indian on horseback to go west. With a nod the scout was on his way.

"They'll find them," Horn said.

"You can go ahead. I have to water these ponies slowly. They're pretty thirsty."

"No, the Apaches can find Yarborough. I'll stay with you."

"Good. I had that varmint treed up in Benito, New Mexico, about three weeks ago. He'd been bullying a small community up there, and I let him go knowing all the time I shouldn't— but I wasn't the law and the people there feared retaliation from him."

"Nice fella."

Slocum gave him half a cigar from his pocket. It was too soon to water the horses again. He struck a match with his thumbnail, and it exploded into flame. Horn drew on his cigar until smoke began to issue out of his mouth around it. Then Slocum lit his half. The powerful nicotine settled him some as both men squatted in the sand and waited.

"That Della is a killer, ain't she?" Horn said, shaking his head as if impressed.

Slocum agreed, and told Horn her story of captivity and becoming a rancher's wife. Then he went and undid the horses and let them have some more water. When they had enough, he took them back and retied them.

"Shame you can't stay up there," Horn reflected.

"More than that, it's a crime." Slocum laughed aloud.

"Man can sure get in some fixes in his lifetime, can't he?"

"And not even try, pard, not even try."

"Why, you've been on the run as long as Jesse James has."

"And made a whole lot less money."

"Yeah, whole lot less." Horn dropped his head, removed his hat, and ran his fingers through his too-long hair. "There ain't always justice in this land."

"Most times you have to buy it, Tom."

"And if it cost a dime, we'd sure never see any of it."

"Right. Those horse of mine looked cooled off enough. I'll give them one more drink and we can ride on."

"Suits me." Horn ground the rest of the butt in the sand and straightened. "We'll ride toward the river. Ben-Gone and the others think that crossing is the one west of here about ten miles."

"You think Loco is headed this way?"

"Good chance, but Captain Eagan's men's horses could never have come this far, so he's guarding the folks at Alma in case Loco doesn't turn south in here somewhere."

"Best he could do from the looks of the horses I saw at the Darby Ranch."

"Pretty pitiful." Horn mounted up, and Slocum finished watering his and then swung up on the gray. They rode down the wash together.

"Whose sorrel?" Horn said.

"Got him on a gambling debt that Forsyth owed me for some time."

"Ought to have made him feel much better getting his debt cleared up since he's dead and all."

Both men laughed. Slocum shook his head. Damn sure had been a hard way to collect money that a man owed him. He still had to sell the horse to come out. Oh, well.

He and Horn stopped at the free-flowing Gila. The south wind swept the sweat from their brows as they watered their mounts. Then they set their ponies loose to graze. He and Horn knelt on the gravel bar, washed their sun-scorched faces, and savored the river's cool healing liquid.

Slocum turned at the drum of a horse.

"That's Pony Boy's horse," Horn said as they struggled to their feet.

Slocum discovered Horn was right when the scout rode in,

and was impressed the man could tell the animal by the sound of the hoofbeats.

"They are west a ways in camp," Pony Boy said in Spanish.

"Bueno Esta hombres?" Horn asked.

"Cīnque."

"Five men including Yarborough," Horn said, turning to him.

Slocum nodded; he knew enough Spanish to survive. "We better take them before Loco arrives."

"Esta Loco?"

The Apache shrugged. He had no idea about the chief's whereabouts either. Horn nodded, then sent him after the others. Obviously he planned a parley before they acted.

"We better do something before dark," Slocum said.

"I agree," Horn said with a worried look. "If we aren't too late already."

Slocum did not want to think about that. But it was a reality.

17

From their vantage point Slocum could see there was a squaw in Yarborough's camp. She was busy tending a cooking fire. He wondered if she was Beckman's. No telling. He was too far away to see if Yarborough was in camp. They had strung a picket line, and several mules were tied along with their saddle horses.

"We made it before Loco did, I'd say."

"Yeah, no telling where he is. Ben-Gone's headed west to see if he can find Loco," Horn said from beside him. The other three scouts were spread out down the hillside watching the campfire smoke swirl along on the ground.

"There's four of them," Horn said, pointing to the men loitering around camp. "You seen Yarborough?"

"No, not yet. You won't miss him. He's big, got a black beard, and loud."

"Damn," Horn swore. "He may have ridden west to meet with Loco. I never thought of that."

"Unless he's hiding. We better take those guns now, before Loco shows up. It would take some time to load them on the mules." Slocum worried more about all the Apaches arriving before they could get away with the weapons.

"What if we bend the barrels or jam them so they aren't usable?"

"Hadn't thought about that." Slocum considered the idea.

Then, if they had to run, the Apaches would have less reason to chase them.

"As long as they can't shoot them, who cares?" Horn said.

"We can use a few of them ourselves, but the rest need to be destroyed. Then they sure won't be of any use to the Apaches." The notion fit their situation. Slocum rolled over on his side and searched the towering hills he'd come over. It would be better if they knew where Yarborough was at, but time was running against them. "When do we start?" he asked Horn.

"I'll send the scouts around. We'll rush them from this side. The scouts will come in from the back and we'll have them in a cross fire."

"Makes sense. There isn't much daylight left." Slocum noted the low-hanging red ball in the west.

"We've got enough time. You use that Spencer to keep them away from those boxes of new rifles and we'll soon have them."

"I can do that," Slocum said.

Horn rose up, bent over in a crouch, and went to tell the scouts their plans. Slocum could see him kneel down and speak to them. They agreed with a nod and soon rushed off to obey his orders. Slocum raised up and studied the camp again. He hoped that Yarborough didn't arrive in the middle of things. He might raise those boys of his up to being fighters.

"We better get in closer range," Horn said, coming back, and the two of them rushed to their horses.

Mounted up, they put spurs to the horses, rounded the wash, and on the flat came on the run. The startled outlaws made a break for their horses.

Good, Slocum thought. He hurried the sorrel, rifle in his right hand, then slipped from the red horse's back and dropped to his knee. He began to pour bullets around the cases of rifles. The dust explosions from his shots convinced the last man to take to his horse.

"They're running!" Horn shouted from his place behind a thick trunk. "Taking tail and skedaddling."

The war cries of Horn's Apaches coming off the hill sent the outlaws whipping and driving across the shallow Gila and up the far side, not looking back in their flight into the junipers.

"Took all the fight out of them," Horn said as they gathered their horses.

A scout reined up and asked Horn about chasing them.

"For a little ways," he said with a grin, and that pleased the Apaches. They booted their mounts toward the river screaming and whooping.

"You got to give them a little fun," he said about his eager wards, and the two of them walked into camp.

Horn spoke in Spanish to the woman and asked her about Yarborough. Slocum could see that long ago someone had cut off her nose for infidelity. The disfigurement did little for her beauty, though she had a shapely body. In her twenties, he guessed. She showed a certain bearing when she moved. The mixture and mingling of Mexican blood from their captives made many of the Indian women very striking. Her name was Nanah.

"He went west," she said. "Never said nothing, except for them to guard the guns." She shrugged and looked at them with sullen eyes.

Horn thanked her and poured himself some coffee.

"Did he kill your man?" Slocum asked her.

She nodded.

"When is Loco coming?" Horn asked, and blew on his steaming drink.

She didn't know.

Slocum glanced down the river's course where it disappeared into the hills and purple mountains. The sun dipped lower, and was about to sink. Somewhere, Loco and his band of renegades were out there. So was Yarborough, and he would be red-hot angry when he discovered the rifles were no longer saleable. The sooner they destroyed the repeaters, the better it would be.

"We need to get to work. Those scouts will be back soon. They can help us," Horn said, then bent over and used his big-bladed knife to pry open the first case.

The heavily greased rifle in his hands, Slocum found a slot between two trees, stuck the barrel in, and proceeded to use

both hands to push on the end of the stock. It was a damn
shame to ruin such good firearms, but something they had to
do. Still, the notion of destroying such weapons made him
sick to his stomach. With some more effort, he felt the barrel
bend. Then he grasped the muzzle and swung it in wide arc.
The walnut stock shattered.

Horn brought over an armful of Winchesters and joined
him. Slocum kept an eye cocked to the west, but saw nothing
in the growing twilight. He didn't want to get so involved in
this destruction they forgot their business.

A rider was coming. He put out his arm to stop Horn, who
nodded that he had heard the same thing. They both drew their
Colts. The woman dropped an armload of weapons with a
clatter and quickly shrank behind them.

It was one of those times, Slocum decided, he'd much rather
be in a feather bed than standing in the twilight, wondering if
it was Loco or Yarborough.

18

"It's Ben-Gone," Horn said, and they holstered their Colts. A wave of relief spread over Slocum. He was anxious to hear what the man had learned. From across the river, the other returning scouts were making the ford. With four more guns, their odds would be a lot better. Ben-Gone reined his sweaty horse up, lithely hopped off, and rushed over.

"What do you learn?" Horn asked.

"Big white man is camped." He motioned over his shoulder. "Some of Loco's men meet him. They will be here in morning."

"All of Loco's men?"

Ben-Gone shrugged. "Don't know. Maybe only send some to get guns."

"We won't be here," Horn said to the scouts, all of whom were now gathered around. "Everyone can take one rifle to keep for himself. The rest we're going to destroy."

"I'll get a pack mule for the ammo," Slocum said, seeing the scouts were busy selecting a rifle. He bent over and took one too. It really made his gut queasy to waste that many good guns, but the plan wasn't bad; the weapons would not fall into the hands of the hostiles this way.

"Enough ammunition there to start a big war," Horn said with a grin.

"If we blow it up they'll know they've got trouble, so we better take it with us." Slocum waited for a reply.

Horn agreed, and Slocum went for a mule. He selected the third one on the picket line that he came to. It didn't spook at his approach. Pads and cross bucks cinched down on the animal, he led it over to the activity. He motioned for one of the scouts to come over and help him load the two panniers of ammunition on the packsaddle.

Their rifle destruction continued with a vengeance. The scouts were having a party.

"They catch any of Yarborough's men?" Slocum asked, joining Horn.

"No, but they scared the hell out of them."

Good enough. Maybe those outlaws wouldn't be back to bother them. Slocum pried open another case with his big knife, and quickly the Apaches destroyed the weapons. At this rate they would be through and on their way in no time. That couldn't be too soon for Slocum; he'd had an itchy feeling in his neck muscles ever since they arrived. Messing with Loco and all his braves was a surefire invitation to suicide.

"Nanah's got some deer stew cooked. We'll eat it, then burn us a trail," Horn said.

"My stomach's been stuck to my backbone for days." Slocum laughed.

"You going with us to Alma?" Horn asked.

"I'll trail along. Need to find Della and make sure she has those new horses and get her safely back to her place."

"If I was you, I'd prop my feet under her table as long as I could."

"Come on, Tom, you've had chances to do that and here you're out running with these scouts and me."

Horn took off his hat and scratched the tousled thatch of his hair on top. "Yeah, I guess you're right. I've just got a natural itch for some adventure all the time. I've tried cow punching and a dozen other things. I get bored as hell."

"Times that I suspect the same thing. Though it would be nice to sit up there awhile at her ranch and enjoy the peace and quiet."

Another rifle stock was shattered against a tree trunk by a whirling scout, and the Apaches laughed out loud. Slocum couldn't see what was funny in the growing dim twilight, but as long as they were breaking them, he could laugh with them.

Nanah's stew wasn't bad-tasting. Had some sand in it that caught in his molars, but he washed that away with her strong coffee. They packed the camp goods on another mule and before the crescent moon rose, they crossed the Gila and headed east. Nanah rode a mule and went along with them like most Apache women, accepting the new situation without a word or comment.

They rode single file until daybreak, and were in the high country by then. The junipers grew taller and pinyons dotted the rims. Slocum led the gray, and planned to switch horses when they rested the next time. Horn headed the train, and a keen-eyed scout watched at the back of the line. Ben-Gone had ridden ahead to be certain the way was clear.

Nothing was taken for granted, but they made good time, trotting whenever the terrain allowed them to. Slocum could see the distant Mogollons, and it made him feel more at ease. A few good hours of sleep and he would feel even better than that. They ate some jerky and crackers at next daylight.

"We keep pushing, we'll be in Alma by late afternoon," Horn promised.

"What'll you do?"

"Tell Captain Eagan where we last saw Loco."

"Not much he can do." Slocum could envision the sorry horses the troopers rode into Darby's. They couldn't go after a desert tortoise if it had a head start.

Horn shook his head. "Not with the horses he has. The Apaches must know how weak they are, making that brazen a drive right into San Carlos even." He shook his head in disbelief. "They knew damn good and well. Loco ain't stupid. He planned it well."

"You think Loco will be satisfied after all this and go back to Mexico?"

"Without the rifles? Maybe, but he probably planned on them." Horn made a grim face. "If you could outguess a fox, you could probably think close to what that old man thinks."

"They talk about Cochise when he was alive, but this one may match him," Slocum said.

"Loco may be the greatest one they ever had." Horn rose

stiffly to his feet "Time to ride. Get your horses," he said in Spanish to the men.

They arrived in Alma before dark. Captain Eagan rushed from his wall tent to greet them. They dismounted and Horn introduced them, and the officer shook Slocum's hand.

"Well, what did you learn?" Eagan asked.

"We learned that Loco is somewhere down on the Gila, but he didn't get the rifles."

"Good. Did you make any arrests?"

"No, they ran like chickens. It's sort of involved."

Eagan looked around as if to be certain there wasn't anyone around close enough to hear him. "Ludman has already filed a report that Loco and his band stole those rifles from his men. They brought in two bodies."

"Forsyth and Beckman?" Slocum asked.

"Yes," Eagan agreed.

"Well, we have the ammunition, and those rifles won't do them bucks any good. We busted them up."

"He'll put in a claim for restitution."

"That's why I knew if we told the local law down there what was happening, they wouldn't believe us," Slocum said with a grim nod. "Excuse me, have you seen Mrs. Hughes?"

"She must still be in Silver City. I sent an armed escort to take her back."

"Thanks. She'll be safe enough there. I'm going to get some sleep and then head that way. Tom, it's been a pleasure. Captain, nice to meet you."

"You are welcome to use my tent," Eagan said.

"Naw, I can find a spot in the shade somewhere and grab a few winks."

"Keep your eyes peeled when you ride south," Tom said after him. "Loco ain't through yet."

Slocum thanked him and led his horses to the water trough. They drank deep. Then he headed for the junipers on the slope. Somewhere up there was a place to sleep until dark. Then he planned to ride to Silver City.

He awoke in the darkness, uncertain how long he'd slept. His horses were grazing; he could hear the chomp of their teeth. They were hobbled and still under the saddles. He'd seen no need to unsaddle them for the short while he'd planned to be there. He rolled up his canvas and blanket bedroll, then tied it on the gray. Horses bridled, he rode off the hillside. The lights of the business district glowed in the night, and he headed for town to buy a couple of cigars—then thought better of it. Might be bounty hunters in the country.

He rode past the welcoming doorways of the saloons. The light from inside cast into the street, and his horses went through patches of yellow. He'd get cigars another time. He gnawed on hard jerky as he went on by.

He reached Gustoff's Crossing on the Gila and nodded to the armed guard on the porch.

"Need to rest my horse," he said to the man in Spanish.

"*Bueno,* help yourself."

He loosened the cinches and let the ponies breathe. It must be past midnight, but he doubted the guard had a watch, so he didn't bother to ask him the time.

"Any problems?" Slocum asked.

"No, it has been very quiet. But Loco, he is still out there."

Slocum agreed, and took a seat on the other high-back chair.

"I remember you now. You were here with the pretty lady, no?"

"Yes. She's in Silver City."

"Ah, yes. I would go there too if she would look at me." The man chuckled at the notion.

"I'll be glad to see her."

"Ah, *sí.*" And the man gave a great sigh.

After what he considered an hour had passed, Slocum remounted and thanked the man, who had rustled up a cup of coffee for him. On the road again by starlight, he pushed south. He hoped to be in Silver City before daylight and not be too obvious when he reached town. The marshal might have received a telegram telling him to hold the man he had, that the other one was misidentified, or by this time Slocum might have been listed as part of the Loco rifle conspiracy. Either way, he planned to make his presence in Silver City less than conspicuous.

At dawn, he hitched his horses in the alley, eased into the hotel lobby, and checked on Della.

"Yes, she is in Room 225," the clerk said.

Slocum held his finger to his lip. "This is a surprise. I'm her brother."

"Oh, yeah," the young man agreed, and Slocum left him.

He hurried up the stairs and soon located her room. He rapped on the door.

"Yes, who is it?"

"Your brother."

"I don't—Slocum!" The door barely cracked, then she threw it open. Then her arms flew around his neck and her wet mouth was all over his.

"Let's get inside and talk," he said in a whisper, searching up and down the hall to see who else took notice of his arrival.

"You are safe. I was so worried. They brought in the bodies of Beckman and that gambler who owed you money."

"Yarborough did that. He intended to sell those rifles to the Apaches and not have to pay for them."

"I had no idea where you were. The horses are coming today. I got the wire. Told them at the telegram office that I was your wife."

"That's fine. What else is going on here? I told the clerk in the lobby you were my sister. Some kind of incest?" He laughed and hugged her. Damn, it felt good to have her back in his arms.

"What do we do?" She nestled her head on his chest.

"Take the horses to Darby. He can surely use the extra ones, as big an operator as he is. We'll cut yours out and take you home. Loco is headed south for Mexico by now. Without his rifles."

"What will you do until the horses come?"

"I'll go up to Gustoff's and meet you there. You should be able to get to there safe enough. I don't think it's healthy for me to stay in Silver City."

"Neither do I, though I don't know a thing. Do you have any money?"

"Some, but I'll be fine."

"Here." She rushed over and found her money pouch, drew the drawstrings, and handed him two double eagles.

"I have some money," he protested. "Got part of my debt back."

"You may need it. Besides, I have charged men on the run that much for one night's stay in the barn and their meals."

"Glad I haven't had to pay to stay there." He gave her a playful spank on the butt.

"Be careful," she said, sounding concerned.

"I will. At Gustoff's Crossing in two days."

She kissed him hard on the mouth, and her blue eyes looked ready to tear. "Please be careful?"

"I will." He pocketed her coins, then stuck his head out in the hall. No one in sight. With a wink and smile, he left her and paused to listen to someone speaking in the lobby. He couldn't make out the words, but he glanced down the hallway and saw the alley exit door.

He waved away her concern, strode down the hall, opened the door, and couldn't see anything out of place in the alley. Two stairs at a time, he reached the alley, then unhitched the horse and mounted. With a last look up, he saw her wave at him, and then he sent the ponies off in a trot. Any minute he expected someone to challenge him. When he reached the street, he turned west, set spurs to the sorrel, and fled Silver City.

He wanted whoever might trail him to think he went west anyway. He tracked back over his prints and generally messed up the pattern until the sun reached noon and he felt certain only an Apache could find him. Then he set out for Gustoff's.

It was long past dark when he arrived and put up and grained his tired horses. Then he went inside to sample some of Mary's cooking. The night guard, Freddie, came in and joined him.

"You didn't find your lady friend?" he asked quietly.

"I did. She's coming. She's bringing some horses for the Darby ranch. I was checking for signs for the Apaches."

"You see any sign of them out there?"

"You heard of anything?" Slocum asked, glancing up when Mary came with the pot.

The man smiled at her. She acted uninterested, refilling his and Slocum's cups with strong steaming coffee. The man waited until she was out of hearing to tell more.

"Loco was mad about some rifles for him that someone busted to pieces."

"Wonder who did that," Slocum said. It never amazed him how much folks knew about things like that—some form of mental telegram. The tame Sioux at Fort Laramie had all fled Squaw Town two days before the post knew that Custer was dead. They had feared reprisals when the authorities learned about the defeat. News had somehow traveled by some telepathy process.

"Who told you he was mad about the guns?" Slocum asked.

Freddie shrugged. "An Apache woman who ran away from his camp."

"She still around here?"

Freddie stole a look around, then under his breath asked, "You want to fuck her? She's not bad-looking."

"No, not that. But I would pay to talk to her. She speak Spanish or English?"

"Come on." The man rose to his feet.

"Wait till I pay for my food and the horses." Slocum wanted to be sure Mary wouldn't think he was leaving without paying her.

"She will trust you."

"I'll pay her first."

Slocum found her in the kitchen. With a coarse cloth she dried her hands, then made him change from a small cash box. In Spanish, she counted the money out loud, and he agreed. He thanked her, pocketed it, and went back to join Freddie.

They hurried out the door. Slocum felt this woman was Freddie's secret, and he wasn't too anxious for anyone to know about her unless there was money involved.

Freddie stuck his head in the doorway of a small hovel and spoke in Spanish. The answer was quiet. Then he stood back and with a head toss invited Slocum to go inside.

Slocum entered and saw the woman squatted at the fire. She looked up, and grinned openly at Slocum. He realized Freddie had not come in. He guessed her to be in her teens, attractive enough in the fire's light. He took a seat on the floor cross-legged.

She wore a blouse of blue material with a deep V in the front. It showed her smooth smoky brown skin and the cleavage of her pear-shaped breasts. The ragged hems of her many skirts were stained with the dust of her travels to escape. She dropped on her butt and hugged her knees.

"You were with Loco?" he asked in Spanish, and she nodded eagerly.

"Was there a big white man there?"

"Much hombre," she agreed.

"Did he stay with Loco?"

She shook her head and pointed to the north. *"Norte."*

"By himself?" he asked.

"Sí."

So he knew that Yarborough was headed away from this region. With Loco rushing south for Mexico, there was no telling where the outlaw would go next. Yarborough would be on the move unless he knew that the two murders were blamed on the renegades and not him. Probably make some long tracks. No matter. Someday their paths would cross again and one of them would not walk away from the encounter.

"Which way did Loco go?"

"Norte."

19

The girl's words struck him like a hard slap. Loco was headed north. Damn, he had to warn Captain Eagan, the people at Darby Ranch, and those Paterson boys. If they all thought the threat was over and let down their guard—he had to get word to all of them or lots more lives would be lost.

Slocum rose to his feet and thanked her. She blinked in disbelief at him.

"You are mad at me?" She scrambled to her feet and rushed to him.

"No, you are beautiful," he said, and pressed a silver dollar in her hand. Then he went outside. His tired horse had many more miles to cover.

"What is wrong?" Freddie asked, and struggled to get up from where he sat.

"I need someone to ride and tell Mrs. Hughes that she is to stay at Silver City. And to keep those horses down there until she hears from me. Loco is not gone to Mexico."

"She told you that?"

"Yes. Why, do you know?"

"No. I mean, she said he wanted to return to Mexico so she ran away."

"He might have wanted to return there, but he's making another circuit north for more raids." Slocum hurried toward the corral with Freddie running beside him. "Who can ride to

142

Silver City tonight and tell Mrs. Hughes to stay there until she gets word it is clear?"

"I can send someone."

"She's at the San Reyes Hotel. But get her word. Loco would steal those horses in a minute and ride clear to Hell on them."

"What are you going to do?"

"Warn the army at Alma and some others." He dug out three silver dollars. "Here's to pay whoever rides to Silver City tonight."

"I will tell her myself, Señor." Obviously that sum of the money was enough to stir up his heroism.

"You have a horse?"

"No."

"Then take my gray," Slocum said, out of fear that the sorrel might be considered as stolen down there. "Don't take long either."

"No. I won't, Señor."

At least he had a square meal in his gut this time, he thought, saddling the sorrel under the stars. Freddie fixed the gray. In a few minutes they were both mounted. Slocum shook his hand with dread. Then he drew himself into the saddle with effort. He had a long ride ahead to make on a tired horse. With a wave, they rode away in opposite directions.

The moon had not come over the Mogollons and the starlight proved weak. Slocum bent over in the saddle and made out a portion of the road's shallow wheel ruts. That and the sorrel's sense would have to get him to Alma.

Late in the night, he found the sleepy camp guard, who bolted up and challenged him.

"Slocum, a friend of Tom Horn's. I need to speak to Captain Eagan."

"We don't disturb him at night."

"This is an emergency. I have information on Loco and he don't know, but he's headed toward here."

"Here?" the private asked in a strangled voice. Obviously no veteran, he started on a run for camp, waving Slocum after him.

"Captain Eagan, sir! Captain Eagan, sir!"

'What the hell's going on out there?" The officer burst out of his tent.

"Slocum, and we ain't got long. Loco's coming back again."

"Oh, Jesus. Excuse me," Eagan said, tucking in his shirt. "When did you learn this?"

"Tonight, from an Apache girl who ran away from his camp. She said he went north after finding those busted-up rifles."

"Damn, he has a day or maybe two on us?"

"I think so. Where is Horn?"

"I think he's sleeping off a bad one."

"Private, come with me. We are going to sober old Horn up."

"Oh, he's mean hung over," the private said.

"A good dunk in that horse tank will take lots of fight out of him," Slocum said. "He needs to be ready to ride in thirty minutes."

'I'll send for his scouts," Eagan called after them.

Slocum signaled he had heard, and the private held back the flap on Horn's tent. He stood at attention and Slocum went by him. Inside the dark interior, Slocum jerked back the sheets and someone female screamed. She grasped the blankets away to cover her nakedness, and Slocum rolled Horn out on the floor.

"Sorry, ma'am, but I need him. Get his feet, Private. Surely you've seen women before?"

"Not her—".

"Never mind. You didn't see her. Get his feet."

'What the hell is going on?" Horn mumbled, his eyes squeezed shut. "Lucy Ann, put me down—ah, baby, put me down."

"We will," Slocum said, and the two raised him over the lip of the tank and doused him in the water.

"Damn you!" Horn shouted, and tried to stand up. Instead the moss-slick bottom went out from under his bare soles and he landed butt-first and splashed water over the sides. Foundering and swinging as if he was in a fight, he reached the side of the tank and grasped the edge.

"You do this, Slocum?"

"No, the cavalry did. Get out and dry off. Loco is back and in our midst."

Horn swept his wet hair back and then shook his head, climbing out in his underwear.

"Shit-fire, and you came all the way back up here to drown me?"

"I'm concerned about Darby's ranch and those boys up there."

"Yeah." Horn scrubbed his mouth with his palm and looked deep in thought. "We'll have to make it up there by foot."

"We better be going then."

"Yes."

"I never thought you could do that and live," Eagan said, joining them with one of his sergeants. Then he chuckled. "They sure dunked you, Horn."

"Oh, hell, we go way back. Captain, could you take those pack mules we got off Yarborough and put enough supplies on them. I think if you would set up an ambush at the Gila crossing, you might catch Loco when he swings back."

"You think he will use that route again?"

"It's the route back to Mexico. He won't stay forever up here. Besides, he's stolen all the horses in the country. He won't find much else left to steal, so in the next few days he'll head south. I'll send Ben-Gone with you. He can set things up and I'll join you as soon as we check out Darby's and Patersons." Horn shook his head. "Man, I won't ever drink that much again."

"Where are you going?" the captain asked.

"With Slocum here to Darby's and those boys that Paterson left up there at that ranch."

"Be careful. Slocum, thanks for all your efforts. I better get all these men around here armed and ready to defend Alma, if I'm going to leave."

"There's plenty of them around here," Horn said, then finished pulling on his pants, which the private had retrieved for him. "Damn, that was a rude awakening. You got one coming from me, Slocum." Then he set off for the rest of his clothing, boots, and guns, walking tenderly on the ground.

A corporal fixed food for them, and the sun came over the

Mogollons. The coffee, bacon, and beans reminded Slocum of his days years before in a gray uniform. Some sorry cook had ruined beans, bacon, and coffee back then too. He tried to forget his meal at Gustoff's Crossing. Mary might have had a little age on her, but even she looked better than the sour-faced corporal who served them. She damn sure made better food.

Horn gulped down his scalding coffee and asked Slocum all kinds of questions.

"When she said north," Slocum explained, "I knew I had to get up here and warn you."

"Why, I'd bet my last dollar that old fox had taken all his treasures and gone south to the Sierra Madres after finding the guns all busted."

"We made him mad, she said."

"I bet we did. Well, lets ride for Darby's." He downed another cup, and his shoulders shuddered when he rose.

"Hot enough?" Slocum asked in disbelief.

"Yeah." Horn breathed and shook his head. "Whew, that was hot as fire."

Slocum, Horn, and three scouts trotted their horse northward on the road. It was past noon when they reached Darby's. Cap Moss came hurrying out of the house.

"Them horses still coming?" he asked, holding his hand up to shade the high sun from his eyes.

"Yes, they're down at Silver City, but we got worse news. Loco is coming back here, we figure. He came up from the Gila west of here and could be close."

"Dang, I figured they were all gone and I sent two boys out to check on the water holes."

"Can you get them back?" Horn asked.

"No, I told them to check several places."

"Pony Boy here can go find them." Horn waved the youngest scout in and spoke to him in Apache. No telling what language he would spout next. Slocum knew the man understood lots that he never divulged in ordinary conversations.

"He'll find your men and get them back if he can," Tom told Caps.

"Good. Them boys ain't real Injun fighters anyway. I

thought Loco was gone from around here or I'd never've done it. Come in and eat. Them scouts too."

Horn shook his head. "They'd like to eat outside. Table manners bother them."

"How's that?" Cap asked.

"They ain't got any." Horn spoke to Pony Boy again and the boy headed for his horse. "Wait. Where's the water holes they're checking on?"

"Over west."

Horn pointed that way, and the boy set out on his smoky gray at a lope.

"He need to eat?" Cap asked.

"Later," Horn said, and closed his eyes for a second as if the headache behind them was making him blind. Slocum did not dare laugh.

They filed in to eat, and several of the cowboys nodded and spoke to them.

"Horn and Slocum came to warn us. Loco ain't left these parts yet."

The sighs and head shakes registered the men's disappointment. Slocum washed his hands before Horn, and then dried them while answering questions of the crew.

"All we know he's retracing some of his old paths up here. We're going to see about the Paterson boys next." Slocum took a seat and bowls of food began to pass his way. He wondered about Mrs. Devon the small children, and the three boys. A bad feeling consumed him and it was deep-rooted. He hoped it was wrong, and reached for the gravy boat.

20

A column of dark smoke sliced the azure sky with the mountains for a backdrop in the north. It made Slocum's stomach churn over and over. The bend in the road rounded the dust-glazed junipers, and he shared a hard look with Horn riding beside him.

"Too damn late," came from Horn's lips, and the look of anger formed a scowl on his face.

"I warned them boys—" The emptiness choked off the rest of Slocum's words.

"It ain't your fault. Let's ride." Horn lashed his horse over and under into a hard burst of speed. Slocum and the two scouts hurried after him down the hard-packed road. With small puffs of dust churned up by their animals' hooves, they pushed toward the inevitable.

Smoke and flames licked the sky from the burning house and outbuildings when they rode into view. Instead of reining up, Horn pushed his horse on harder. Slocum charged on his heels. A little caution might not be bad. He undid the thong that held down his Colt, and felt the sorrel give his best effort to catch up. He dismounted in a sliding stop at the first body. Colt in hand, Slocum knelt and turned over the stripped-naked body of the youngest Paterson boy. Blue eyes stared at the empty sky, the life in them lifted.

Gawdamnit. Why did they have to castrate and mutilate him? He was an innocent boy; didn't deserve such treatment.

Slocum turned away and looked for Horn, who had ridden beyond the burning house that crackled in flames. The roof crashed into the inferno consuming it. Hell—he knew this would happen. Without anything to cover his body with, Slocum shut the boy's eyelids and then turned his limp body over to hide the devastation.

Horn came back on foot around the great funeral pyre of the dwelling. The grim set of his jaw told Slocum he'd found no survivors.

Then Slocum heard a cry, and one of the scouts came carrying a small boy in his arms. The kid's face was black with soot and tears of fear running down his cheeks. The scout gave him to Slocum.

He guessed the boy to be about three. He wore some ragged pants and a small pullover shirt. His hair was singed, and he smelled like he had pooped in his britches, but the fact that he was alive made Slocum smile.

"Where did you find him?" Slocum asked the scout in Spanish.

"Chickens."

Slocum figured that was the chicken house, or someplace the boy had gone off to to explore, missing the raid.

"What is your name?" he asked, standing him on his feet.

"Poopy," he said, then reached behind at his soiled pants with a disappointed look.

That was never going to do for a real name. Surely he had a name and could say it. No telling what he had seen and experienced. Obviously the Apaches had missed him.

"It's going to be okay, Brigham," Slocum said, and took his hand.

"Name's not Brigham."

"Good, tell me your name."

"Taylor."

"Good name. Let's take you down there and wash you off." Slocum turned to Horn. "Can him and I go down to the tank and not see anything too bad?"

"Yeah. The others are around the other side of the house. I think one of the boys was inside the house."

"All dead?"

"Yeah. It ain't pretty."

"I'll wash him up some. Then we can go."

"Let's go back to Darby's. I've got the scouts looking for signs of what way they're headed from here. No need to stay out here and risk some of them swinging back by, though I think they're gone this time."

Slocum stripped the sniffling boy down, then washed his smeared behind and looked for a rag to dry him. Horn brought a sack for a towel, and Slocum thanked him.

"Where's Mamma?" Taylor asked.

"She's gone. You and me are going to take a ride when we get through here."

"I want her."

"Taylor, she's gone for a very long trip." Slocum finished drying him and made a swipe at his face.

"Don't. I want her." He turned around and around looking for her.

"Come on, Taylor. You and me are going to go see the captain. You know him? Well, you are in for big treat, pardner." He hoisted the boy into the saddle and then swung up behind him on the seat.

"You hold that horn tight," he instructed, and they started out of the yard.

"Believe he's going to make it. Some things just ain't fair, are they?" Horn asked, riding in beside him.

"Nope." Things never worked out that way. Satisfied the boy was going to ride all right, they set into a trot. They had lots of miles to cover.

Past dark they reached Darby's, and the cowboy standing guard nodded to them.

"See anything?" he asked.

"They already did their damage," Horn said. "Before we got there."

"All of them?"

"Except a young boy. Slocum's got him there."

"Oh, hell," the cowboy said, sounding upset. "I wonder about Squirt and Bailey now."

"Pony Boy's not back yet?"

"No. We thought he'd go find you and then join you, instead of coming back here."

"Shit!" Horn said out loud.

"What is it?"

"That boy would have come back here by dark, bad as a damn Apache hates the night."

"You thinking Loco got him?"

"I'd sure bet that way. Oh, hell, I should have sent one of them older ones."

"Like I should have made Mrs. Devon and them Paterson boys come up here to Darby's?" They reined up at the porch.

"What have we got here?" Cap asked, taking the sleeping child from Slocum.

Relieved of his burden, Slocum flexed his cramped arm back and forth. Times like this, there was no answer to who was responsible for what. Poor Taylor had lived, when the rest were dead.

"Get down. We have food. Where are the scouts?" Cap asked.

"They're looking for where Loco went," Horn said, and dismounted heavily. Slocum did the same, and his legs threatened to fold under him. It was hard to find them. He hung on the saddle horn and closed his eyes. He'd had enough dead and dying to last him, and it wasn't over yet.

They washed up and dried their sunbaked faces. Slocum was unsure his upset stomach could even consider food. He went through the motions and filled his plate with beef, rice, and beans.

"What're you going to do with that boy?" Cap asked.

"Take him to his father in Silver City." Slocum said.

Cap nodded. He had put the boy on a blanket spread on the floor, and Taylor slept. Lots of innocence lying there. He didn't even know what had happened to his mother or the rest of his family. Somehow he would go on with his life.

"Well, what else did those bloody bastards do?" Cap asked.

"You don't want to hear," Horn said. "We didn't bury them. Figured we'd get the boy back here and maybe have some answer about your men."

"That scout never returned here. What do you figure happened to him?"

Horn shook his head warily. "It ain't real good that Pony Boy isn't back here. He's young, but he's dependable."

"What's the damn army doing about Loco?" Cap demanded.

"They have tried to head him off," Slocum said. "They left Alma on foot."

"But—what the hell else could they do?" Cap dropped his head in defeat.

"Captain Eagan gets there before Loco makes that crossing, he'll sure stop him and hurt him bad."

"On foot?" Cap raised an eyebrow and then dismissed the idea.

"Those soldiers are tough," Horn said. "They want him stopped too."

"I want to change the subject," Slocum injected. "Those Texas horses are at Silver City and Della Hughes wants some. There will be maybe twenty head over. You want them?"

"I'll need all of them. We'll be a while regathering those cattle again. Once those three- and four-year-old longhorn steers figure you out, they get real skittish the second time."

"Good. I told her to wait there until we were certain that Loco couldn't steal them."

"You did real well to do that." Cap gave a nod of approval. "That would be all I need. I'll send two men down there to help drive them up here."

"Good idea. I'll take the boy to his father in Alma tomorrow." Slocum put down his fork. Trying to eat was not working. "What about you, Tom?"

"I'll go look for Pony Boy and gather up my scouts. We need to be at the Gila crossing with the captain, but I think we're already too late."

"Why's that?"

"A hunch is all. Even if he ran smack dab into Captain Eagan, Loco could dodge around him quick and be gone again. The captain can't chase him. I better head that way and see what I can do to help him."

"We'll have breakfast at first light," Cap said. "You and Horn take a remuda horse in the morning. Yours are done in.

We have the horses we rode in on, and with more coming I'll have enough. That's the least I can do for you two."

"Thanks."

"Yeah, thanks." Slocum nodded at Horn. Good man, Captain Moss. The West needed more men like him.

With the little boy under the Mexican housekeeper's care, the pair went to sleep in the bunkhouse. Slocum didn't care— he wanted some sleep and lots of it. Maybe when it was all over, he could hibernate the rest of the year. He checked the stars overhead and the growing crescent moon.

"In Georgia, it would rain out of that shape of a moon," he offered to Horn.

"In Arizona and New Mexico, somebody might piss on the ground under it," Horn joked.

"Yes," Slocum said, then stepped to the corral and undid his fly. He planned to make Horn's prophecy come true.

Somewhere a Mexican red wolf howled. More mournful and deeper than any song-dog ever managed. Then a mate answered, and they swept away after some deer they hoped to pull down before morning. Like the wolf and the Apache, he too was hunted. They had no place in this land for any of them—maybe in a side show cage, on a reservation, or behind bars. The sentence hung over them all.

"You coming to bed?" Horn asked, breaking into his thoughts.

"Yeah, in a minute. Go ahead."

21

"You mean—" The man paled at the news of his family's death and looked too weak to take the child. Slocum shifted the boy around in his arms; the good Darby horse between his knees moved too.

"They are all dead," Slocum said in a voice that trailed off. He didn't know if the Paterson boys' mother was in the gathering crowd or not.

"The Paterson boys—they're dead?" someone asked.

Slocum nodded, and handed the baby down to a stout-looking woman who came forward to take him. Then dismounted heavily.

"Poor thing won't ever know his mother," the woman said, and the boy struggled to be put down. At last, she set him down. He ran back and hugged Slocum's leg.

"He likes you," someone commented.

Mrs. Paterson came screaming. "Not my boys! Not my boys!"

Slocum bent down and hoisted Taylor in his arms. He hated to face her worse than anything. He could recall the concern she'd shown for her sons. If only they'd listened to him and not let down their guard, maybe they would have lived. Then again, maybe not.

"Ride the horsie, ride the horsie," Taylor said.

"Not now, son," Slocum said softy.

"Tell me it isn't true! Dear God, tell me!" the distraught woman cried.

"They're dead, ma'am." He patted Taylor on the head as the boy clung to his neck. It would be hard to separate from him, but Slocum had to.

He squatted down and caught the wet-eyed boy's look as he set him on his knee. "Taylor, you have to go with that lady. I have horses to go get and things to tend to. She's probably got some food. Good food."

The boy tried to hug him, but Slocum was forced to hold him back.

"Taylor, I'll be back to see you, pard. You have to go with her."

"Ride the horsie," he pleaded.

Slocum lifted him up and handed him to the woman. "Sorry, he ain't listening."

"Oh, he'll be fine and thank you, mister. You sure have done a good job with him."

"Not good enough," he said, and remounted. It cut him deep to look back at those pleading brown eyes and small out-stretched arms. Then he turned Darby toward Silver City. That was the name he'd christened the big bay with, Darby. It felt good to have a stout horse beneath him again.

Darby was muscled, conditioned, probably five or six years old, and Slocum could sense he wouldn't buck. He wore a number two shoe, had enough hoof to support his muscular body, and was long enough that he didn't ride choppy. He stood perhaps fourteen hands high at the withers, not a tall horse, but from his conformation, his veins carried some Texas Steel Dust blood, and most of those good using horses never reached over fifteen hands tall.

Slocum stopped at the saloon, went inside, and bought a few cigars. He waved off the offer of a beer and went back out in the sunshine. Stopping on the porch to light a smoke, he studied the sun-filled street, busy with commerce and children rushing about playing tag with endless energy. He was anxious to find Della Hughes. Time to get on with his life.

On the road, he caught up with the ranch hands headed for Silver City to help drive the horse herd up there. The three of them rode at a long trot, and reached Gustoff's Crossing in the afternoon.

"Better put up here," Slocum said. "It's still a ways to Silver City."

He spotted his friend Freddie, and they had a short visit. Yes, the fine lady was staying in Silver City until he came or sent word. He thanked the man and put Darby in the corral. Then he and the other cowboys headed for the main structure and some food.

"Oh, Señor!" Freddie called. He hurried over to tell him. "They say that Loco is back in Mexico."

"Good. Did the army try to stop him?"

"Yes, it was big battle and Loco lost some men, they say. But the 'Paches went around them and the army had no horses to pursue them."

"Thanks. Good to know." Slocum wondered as he walked on if Tom Horn had made it there in time to fight.

"Who in the hell told him that?" one of the cowboys asked, looking back with a scowl at Freddie as they walked.

"Maybe a magpie," Slocum said. "News can travel fast in this country."

"We never heard about no battle at Alma."

"That bartender didn't have an Apache wife either."

"He have one?" the cowboy asked.

"Yeah."

"Gawdamn, I'd be afraid every night she'd cut my throat," the cowboy said.

"Or your balls," the second puncher chimed in.

"You boys ain't lived till you shared your blankets with Apache women," Slocum baited them.

"You done that?"

Slocum nodded and drew a deep breath. He wished he had a dime for every time. No, that would be bragging, but he had spent some fine times in bed with copper-skinned women.

The next afternoon they arrived at Silver City. He let the cowboys go into town without him on the excuse that he and the marshal didn't see eye to eye. They accepted that and went on in. So Slocum scouted around until he found the horse herd out grazing and met Tuffy Brome, the ramrod. He was a wiry bronc-twister type with bull-hide chaps, a droopy-brim Boss of the Plains hat, and a mustache that resembled a ten-year-old longhorn's rack. He kept it twisted tight. With a Texas drawl, he invited Slocum to drop down and join him for some coffee.

"That sounds good," Brome said after Slocum finished telling him that Loco was supposed to be in Mexico and the two Darby cowboys were going to help trail the herd north.

"Been an easy trip so far," Brome said, and poured him some more coffee. "That Mrs. Hughes is some lady." He shook his head as if impressed. "I reckon that's your brand on her?"

"I don't reckon she has a brand," Slocum said. "Della is a real lady."

"Well, that's powerful, but she sure speaks highly of you."

"Got her fooled is all."

Brome cut him a look that showed he didn't believe that either, and they settled on the ground and enjoyed the break in the warm sun.

"You're welcome to stay with the outfit," Brome said.

"I'll do that. Me and the law a while back had a little altercation in Silver City," Slocum said, assuming the man would understand.

"I know about them deals myself. Won't no one in this outfit tell him you're here."

"Obliged." Slocum sat cross-legged, savored the strong coffee, and looked over the herd of roans, bays, blacks, and sorrels grazing out across the flats. It felt good to just sit without a million things buzzing in his head.

Loco was back in the Sierra Madres. Slocum had been there. He knew the endless canyons, the peaks that held snow most of the year, and the thin trails that led to and through them. The icy streams teemed with silver trout and the fat mule deer with tall racks bounded across the clearings. But where had Yarborough gone? North, so the Apache girl had said, but that was not even a definite direction. Their paths would cross again and he wouldn't let him off the next time. Slocum drank the rest of his coffee, then beat the grounds out of his cup.

• • •

Della arrived at the herd on a lathered horse an hour later. She dismounted and rushed to hug and kiss him.

"Oh, I was so worried about you."

"I was fine."

"Yes, but I didn't know anything until those cowboys came and told me."

"Doing fine," he said, looking down into her fresh face and wishing they were alone in her cabin or in some secluded mountain hideout.

"The cowboys say we can head for home in the morning," she told him.

"Yes, and Cap Moss wants the extra horses too. He has a hard roundup facing him."

"Wonderful. We can be home in four days. Can't we?"

"I don't know why not."

"Oh, the marshal asked me about you. I told him you'd gone up to Utah. They wired him back the next day for him to hold you until the Abbott brothers arrived. Seems that the fella someone brought back from Colorado wasn't you."

"Them or that Texas bounty man around town?"

"I haven't seen them."

"Good."

"What are you thinking?"

"I better ride up that way and join you later on the trail."

"Oh." She made a pained face of disappointment.

"Hey, I feel the same way, but I don't need you caught in some crazy gunfight. We'll have time together, I promise, when we get back to your place. Lots of it."

"Good. You be careful."

"You do the same." He kissed her on the mouth, and at the same time considered himself the stupidest man on earth, leaving such a wonderful opportunity and with her all primed.

He thanked Brome and rode north. He reached Gustoff's Crossing after dark, ate a meal, and bedded down in an empty adobe hovel. Sometime in the night, he heard voices. Loud ones. His hand closed on the redwood handle of his Colt, and he stood up in his stocking feet trying to determine the source and their purpose. It was pitch black and he could hear them arguing.

They were headed for the main building. Quickly he sat down on the bed and pulled on his boots. Something niggled him about the voices. His footgear on, he strapped on his Colt, and blinked when a shadow slipped in the room. It was the Apache girl.

"Vamoose, hombre," she said upon discovering him awake.

"That's the law came in?" he asked her in Spanish.

"Sí. Freddie said for you to hurry and go. They look for you."

"Gracias," he said, and handed her a dollar.

She stepped in close, and he could smell the aroma of woodsmoke and the musk of her body. With her free hand she ran her palm over his crotch and then nodded.

"You come back sometime. I will show you where to put it."

"I bet you would," he said, and gave her a hug.

He gathered his bedroll and kack. He tried to see if the men were still at the main building, but they weren't in sight—probably eating. Satisfied, he headed out the doorway. She trailed along with him, keeping a lookout while he bridled Darby and saddled him. When he finished, she opened the gate and let them out.

"Vaya con Dios," she said softly, and he gave her a peck on the cheek. Her hand flew to her face where he'd kissed her, but he could see her wide grin in the starlight.

"Same to you," he said.

He swung in the saddle and headed up the road. Whoever they were, they were looking for him. He breathed a sigh of relief. A good thing he hadn't stayed with the horse herd. For one thing, he still remembered the Silver City jail's stinking outhouse—the foul smell and the buzzing flies were all too vivid in his mind. He set Darby into a trot. The moon would soon be coming up over the Mogollons. Then he glanced back, saw no pursuit, and rode on.

22

He rode into Alma in the early morning, and stopped at the
saloon, had a beer, and ate some boiled eggs and crackers from
the free-lunch board. Then, with a few more cigars in his vest,
he set out again. He reached the Darby place in mid-morning.
Cap came out of the house. His eyes were red, probably from
bookwork that he must have been toiling over.

"Your horses are coming," Slocum said. "Had a little deal.
I needed to come ahead."

Cap merely nodded as if he didn't care. "We been burying
a lot of folks. Them two hands was murdered and that Apache
scout too. We also put them Paterson boys and Mrs. Devon
and her two kids to rest. Been quite a funeral party." He shook
his head in disapproval. "Gawdamn, this was good country.
All this killing and I don't know—I grew up fearing Comanches in Texas, and I come out here and there's more heathen
killers out here than there was at home."

"It's about over," Slocum said. "Loco made his last desperate raid up here."

"Sure hope you're right. I had to write those hands' families. Tough deal."

"Cap, I come by to be honest with you. I can't honestly
take this good horse in trade for that colt."

"The hell you can't. Why, the colonel himself would have
given you that horse. If that's all you've got to say, ride on."

"I wanted to hear you say that. My conscience won't bother

me again. By the way, Brome is bringing you some great horses. I saw them down there."

"Appreciate it. Ride careful. You ever need a haven, come by and stay a spell. We're tight-lipped around here about our friends."

"I will sometime. Cap, see you. If you would, tell Mrs. Hughes I'll be along." Cap nodded, and Slocum turned Darby for the gate. He planned to meet Della up at her place. Then he could decide if anyone was still on his backtrail.

Two days later, he reached her outfit. He didn't ride in the front way, but skirted around to the back side. Standing in the stirrups, he checked the pens for any sign of an animal in them. He dropped off the saddle, left Darby ground-tied to graze, and searched around the barn for boot-heel marks. He saw nothing, and unsaddled his horse and put his kack in the barn; everything looked untouched.

The next few days he kept the new Winchester handy while he cut and split firewood. Instead of sleeping in the cabin, he used his bedroll on the ground near the sheds. If they were coming up the spine looking for him, he wanted to be ready. With Darby in the corral, he could look up from his chores and see if the horse noticed anything. Horses could see and smell things that humans couldn't, and made good sentinels.

So he rolled his shoulders into the whack of the ax and the seesaw action of the big-toothed crosscut all day. By sundown, he was ready for his bedroll, his nose full of the smell of split pinyon, juniper, and some oak and his tight muscles crying for a stretching. Her winter woodpile grew taller, and soon he had all the logs she had dragged in cut up, and considered going after more.

Then he heard a bell horse coming from the south, and snatched up the rifle. In a short while her familiar hat appeared and she came driving her dozen ponies. By then he was sitting on the porch, hat down over his head and pretending he had been resting the whole time.

He rose and stretched, then angled off the porch to open the pen for her.

"Good-looking horses," he said.

"Nice pile of wood," she said before she dismounted.

"Oh, I guess some beaver came by and did that."

"He's been a damn busy one." She slapped her horse on the butt and sent it in the corral. Then she crowded close to him and used her thumb to push her hat back off her head to catch on the string around her neck.

They kissed. Words weren't necessary. Two hungry faces fed off each other. Consumed with their needs, they rushed inside the house, toed off boots, stripped away their clothing, then became one on top of the high-piled feather mattress.

He trembled finding her. His hips ached to pound her. Then she cried out when he opened her gates. Filled with their heady pent-up desires, they fought to reach the fiery inferno of their wildest passion. Her contraction inside began to strip him, and the aching in his scrotum built to overwhelming force until he drove as deep inside her as he could and then exploded. They both fell in a pile and slept as one.

It was dark when they stirred. Groggy and depleted, she slipped into a robe and some slippers. Excusing herself, she went outside to use the facilities out back. He pulled on his canvas pants, decided he needed the same relief, and started out the door. Then came the blow on his head—for an instant he saw two men holding her, the fear in her eyes, and after that all went blank.

Slocum found himself tied, facedown. The rough-hewn log flooring was abrasive on his bare chest and the night's cold made a shiver run up his spine. Where was Della and who had hit him over the head? All that time they must have been watching him. But if they were lawmen or bounty hunters, why didn't they—

Where was everyone? He finally forced himself to his feet and staggered to the door. It was open. He listened. Someone was sobbing somewhere. Were they gone? He shook his dizzy head. Too damn dark to see much. He blinked his eyes, then back in the dimness saw her white hand tied to the bedpost.

"You all right?" he asked in a voice more hoarse than he'd expected.

"Oh, Slocum, I thought they killed you," she cried.

"I'm fine. Who was it?" He eased himself over to the dry sink to search for a knife.

"Said he was Yarborough and you owed him. You all right?"

"I'm fine. Looking for a knife." He knocked over a tin plate, and it rang like a bell on the floor. "How long they been gone?"

"Not long. Oh, I'm sorry—" She began to bawl.

"Ain't your fault. We're alive."

"Oh, Gawd, those bastards—"

"They'll pay for it, honey. They'll pay for everything." They would rue this day if he had to search the face of the earth for them. He found the knife, but cutting the rawhide was not easy with his hands tied too. With all the patience he could muster, he fought it until at last the tight bounds came loose and the knife clattered to the floor. He stripped the rawhide bands from his wrist, then knelt down and sought the knife by feeling for it.

He carefully cut her right hand loose, then leaned over, discovering her naked when he slashed the left one free. She bolted up and buried her face in his chest. His eyes squeezed shut in dismay at her fate, and he tossed the knife aside. It bounced on the floor beyond the bed, and he hugged her tight. She cried for some time despite his attempts to soothe her feelings.

"I guess they robbed you too?" he said.

"Only the money I was carrying. They didn't know I had any more."

"Good. Can you recall the names of the others?"

She squeezed him. "I heard one called Mica."

"Good enough."

"You're not going to leave me, are you?"

"Yarborough will hurt someone else tomorrow. He's got to be stopped." Slocum stared hard at the moonlight streaming in the open doorway. He had to stop them; they would go on robbing and raping until someone did.

"But what will you do against that many?"

"Were there three of them?"

"Yes, I can't—"

"Was the other one's name Dash?"

"I think so. He was just a boy. Oh, Slocum, I haven't felt this filthy since——"

"The Apaches?"

"Yes."

"What did Hughes teach you?"

"Hold your head up no matter what."

"You do that."

"You're going to leave me in the morning, aren't you?"

He simply nodded his head and hugged her tight. He would be gone come daybreak. They needed enough time so they would decide he was not coming after them. That impulsive urge to rush in would be what they expected. He knew better than to do that—just dog them until the time was right.

At daybreak, her eyes red from crying, she stood beside him at the corral. She forced a small pouch of money inside his shirt and refused to take it back.

"You will need that before this is over," she said.

"Thanks. I'll be back by and by."

She nodded, but didn't look at him. "I've hired that boy Tad who came here with Randy. I need someone. He told me he never did anything bad in his life but borrow one horse up in Utah. Kinda got caught up and he thought Randy was going to show him a better life. He said it hadn't happened."

"Good. You need help here."

"Slocum, he ain't going to live in my house——"

"Della, you need a man. He makes one, marry him."

"You're a son of bitch at times, Slocum."

"Time to be honest with each other."

"I know, I know—you will be careful."

"That boy coming soon?"

She nodded stiffly. "He's bringing some supplies on two pack mules. I fixed it up so he couldn't leave down there for a couple of days. So you and I—well."

"Keep your chin up, girl."

"I'm trying."

Slocum nodded and, satisfied with his cinch, mounted and waved to her. No time to stay any longer, or he'd never leave. That boy would take care of her, or she'd take care of him.

He drew a deep breath and nodded to himself. His right hand sought the butt of the Winchester in the scabbard and he set Darby into a lope.

He couldn't look back; didn't dare.

23

A sheepherder told him of three men riding north the day before. The descriptions fit Yarborough and his crew. Satisfied, Slocum thanked the old man and pushed Darby on at a long jog. He had no intention of catching them, not yet. Ahead of him lay the open high country. He let the bay pick his way down the steep slope. They were going toward Navajo and Hopi country. It made no difference. He planned to find them when they least expected it.

He rode up the streets of St. Johns and paused. A dead body lay in the back of a buckboard. Most corpses were covered out of respect. This one wasn't, and he wanted to check it.

He looked at the closed eyes of Dash. He had still a youthful palor on his ivory-white face, with the thin peach fuzz he'd tried to grow into a beard.

"You know him?" a man with a star on his vest asked.

"Seen him before," Slocum offered, reining Darby back a step.

"John Doe is all I know."

"What got him killed?"

"Got in an argument with a teamster about a wagon across the street. Hell, he could have rode around. Drew a gun on the man. Another teamster drilled him."

"He by himself?"

"Near as I can tell. I was in court and heard the shooting,

but it was all settled by the time I got down there. You got a moniker to put on him?"

Slocum shook his head. "No, I don't." He touched his hat brim and rode on. One down, two to go.

His next destination was the Little Colorado crossing. An outpost considered tough by many and where a storekeeper had sent him to look for them. "If they're headed north, that's the crossing they'll go over," he'd said. "Watch yourself. Some tough ones hang out up there."

Slocum had thanked him, pocketed his cigars, and ridden north. A few showers sprinkled him while he rode; then they swept off to the Grand Canyon in the northwest. The drizzle hardly deserved unfurling his slicker for it. He rode on, stopping a family of Navajos and asking them if they'd seen someone fitting Yarborough's description.

They shook their heads and in their brief, halting Spanish told him no. Slocum thanked them and rode on. He arrived at the crossing and stopped by the trading post.

"No, Señor, there has been no one like that in here this week."

"*Gracias,*" he said, and paid the man for the canned tomatoes, cheese, and crackers he'd bought to eat on the trail.

He went outside to sit on the bench. With his jackknife he speared holes in the can top to drink the juice. He'd drunk enough gyp water coming up there, and he was anxious to get to the acid liquid in the can. Someone slipped up and sat beside him.

He looked over at her velvet blouse and the flash of the silver around her neck. She was Navajo. He waited for her to say something, but she looked straight ahead, so he raised the can and let the tangy fluid fill his dry mouth. Heavenly. At last, he quit drinking and wiped the back of his hand over his mouth. Nothing better in the world than canned tomatoes.

"Those two men came by here," she said in English.

"Huh?" he asked in a low voice.

"Those two men came by here yesterday."

"The ones I asked him about in the store?"

"Yes."

"Why did he say no?"

She shook her head. "Maybe you are the law?"

He paused, ready to drink some more of the juice. "No, I'm not. Where did they go?"

"They were talking. I heard them say they needed to go see a man called Benito."

"No, that's a village." The tomato juice began to roil around in his belly. He felt ready to puke, and had to force it down hard behind his tongue. He must be three hundred miles or more from there, but he had to stop them.

How would they go there? He had to be waiting for them somehow when they arrived. What could he do? Maybe ride the train to Sante Fe, take the stage north to Taos, and get a horse. He might even beat them there.

He dug in his pocket and found her a silver dollar. She smiled and dropped it down the front of her blouse. "We could go in back?" she offered in a low voice.

"No, next time. I must leave."

"You aren't a lawman, are you?"

"No, I'm not."

He rode Darby hard back to St. Johns. He arrived with little sleep and sold the bay for twenty-two dollars, a cheap price. But it amounted to twice the cost of a one-way ticket on the Atlantic and Pacific Railroad to Sante Fe.

He arrived at the Sante Fe depot, then took a buggy ride to town with several well-dressed matrons who'd also disembarked from the train.

In Santa Fe, he booked stage passage to Taos, and learned he had time to eat some tamales from a street vendor. In fact, the stage was not leaving for three hours. So after he finished his lunch, he ducked inside the Elephant Saloon, and won enough money at poker in the next two hours to cover his living expenses for three months. He left there in adequate time to take his seat on the stagecoach. He climbed aboard and then looked back at the gray elephant painted on the front facade across the square. He'd had more success at cards than his last time in this town.

The driver shouted, and nearly unseated him and the other passenger, a drummer, when the team bolted ahead.

"Wait! Wait!" someone shouted. Slocum sought his seat and

pushed himself back off his boots until his back was in place, bracing himself for the man's wild driving.

"What in the blasted hell for?" demanded the driver.

"A lady has a ticket for this trip."

"Sorry, ma'am."

"It's fine. Sorry I am late." She climbed inside, looked twice at the space beside Slocum, who was facing the back, and then took her place.

He guessed her to be in her thirties. Mexican blood, but aristocratic. She was no Indio. Maybe pure Spanish. Her dark blue cape was made of expensive material. From what he could see of her tight-fitting dress, it was very fashionable. The hat she wore hid most of her face, and when she unpinned it, Slocum felt grateful. In the next twelve hours he planned to enjoy his ride looking at her beauty whenever the chance arrived.

"Margarita Estancia."

"Slocum," he said as she busied herself undoing her cape.

"Slocum? What nationality is that?"

"Georgia."

She shook her head. "You can't be that."

"People who come from Mexico are Mexican. I am Georgian."

"Like me, Señora. I am a Kentuckian," the drummer in the opposite seat said.

"I am not a señora." She shook her head in dismay at the peddler seated opposite her. Her cold gaze was enough to make him turn away and put back on the bowler hat he'd tipped at her.

"You are playing a game with me, no?" she asked Slocum directly.

"I am more Georgian than anything else."

"You are a cattleman?"

"No."

"No?" She looked disappointed. "What do you do?"

"Freight, drive cattle, do errands for folks."

"Ah, you a *pistolero* then?"

"Sometimes."

"How much would you charge to kill someone. Like if I

wanted him killed?" She pointed her finger at the drummer. The man frowned and slunk down in the seat.

"Different prices."   •

"A hundred in gold?" She pointed her finger at the man and said, "Bang." The man jumped.

"I don't consider—" the drummer protested.

She waved his complaint away. "We aren't killing you yet. Would you kill him for a hundred in gold?" she asked Slocum.

"What for?"

"Oh, you have to have reason, huh?" She made an impatient face at him.

"It's always better to have a reason."

They swept through the valley, and junipers boughs brushed the coach on both sides. Dust boiled up. From his side window, he could see the towering snowcapped peaks. This trip would be a pleasant one as long as Margarita Estancia rode alongside him.

"Let's say he stole my honor. Then would you kill him?"

"He hasn't done that or he would be crowing like a banty rooster."

"Ah, yes, you could tell that, huh?"

Slocum glanced over and saw a flush of embarrassment on her smooth cheeks. The lady was not as worldly as she obviously acted. Though he found her very demanding, obviously she was a member of a very rich family. Why wasn't she a señora? He would need to know the reason why not.

The coach ran downhill, the evergreen-clad land opened into grassland, and they passed many ox carts lumbering along piled high with various goods going to Sante Fe. Loads of sacked grain, peeled poles for housebuilding, adobe bricks, hay, and produce from the valley ahead.

At the first change of horses, he helped her down and she hurried for the facilities out back. He knew not to drink much before a stage ride or face a bloated bladder. Nonetheless, he sauntered around to the men's facility and used it. Then he waited for her return. The drummer came past him.

"That woman's a contrary bitch," he said.

When the man was halfway inside the coach, Slocum said very loudly, "Bang."

The man whirled around. "You ain't funny either."

"Maybe you should catch the next coach going north," Slocum said.

"I've got rights."

"I've got a ten-dollar gold piece says you can't make that much in three days wherever you're going."

"Give it here. Be good damn riddance to the both of you." The man's fist grabbed the coin and he almost ran right into her.

"He's leaving?" she asked with a frown.

"Health reasons," Slocum said. "He was afraid your finger would be loaded next time."

She smiled, pleased at Slocum. "I see why people hire you. You get things done. I would have hated for him to ogle me all the way up there."

"So would I, so I'll do twice as much," Slocum said, and followed her into the coach.

"And where is your wife?" She turned and faced him despite the jerk as the coach started up and the grumbling of the driver about damn passengers changing their minds.

"Don't have one. In my business I am never in one spot too long."

She put her hand under the side of her cheek and looked him over speculatively. He had a feeling of being measured and undressed. He studied the small grassy hills, and then turned back to look at her pouty lips.

"You aren't married?" he asked.

"No."

"Why not? You must have a dowry big as this stagecoach."

"Are you saying I am an old maid?" Her dark eyes turned to coal.

"Too attractive to be that, I would say."

"Oh, now I am a pretty old maid."

Slocum had had all he could stand, so he leaned over and kissed her. Her lips were soft and poised. Despite the rough pounding of the coach, he was pleased with his ten-dollar investment. While her lips moved under his, he sought her rock-hard breast under the dress material and the stiff corset. He soon curled his fingers and eased them inside the corset's shell. Their kisses grew longer and steamier.

She breathed faster and faster. His hand disengaged, and he sought to go under her dress and feel the silk stocking, but she quickly pulled his hand free.

Out of breath and looking pale, she shook her head and straightened up. "I am sorry. I am a virgin and I have misled you. It was terribly wrong for me to do this." She swallowed hard and then ran her red tongue along her lips. "You must understand?"

He nodded. His head was about to split with the urgency driving him. He drew in his breath plotting his next move. She had to—

"Maybe this will help you," she said, and dropped to her knees on the floor, adjusted her dress, then moved between his legs. Her fingers undid his gunbelt and pushed it back. Then she undid his suspender buttons. Biting her lower lip, she began to undo his fly. It took all his willpower to sit there while she peeled it back. Then, as if he wasn't even present, she undid his underwear, curled her index finger around his cramped erection, drew it out, and popped it into her hot mouth.

He slouched down and closed his eyes and hoped Taos never came.

24

"I have a horse for you to ride," she said, cuddled up in his arms in the growing darkness. Clouds shrouded the setting sun as the rocking stage rushed northward over the tablelands, headed for the sleepy town of Taos at the base of the mountains.

"I might not be able to return him."

"Ah, but I could give him to you. Then perhaps someday you would ride by again."

"And if he died?"

"Oh, well, I have many horses." She snuggled her head tighter to his chest.

"What would your father say?"

"Silly girl, if you give a drifter a horse, of course he will ride away with it," she said in a falsetto bass voice. "Why don't you marry some old man I choose for you who is rich and wants you?"

"Oh, so he has some rich old man picked out for you?"

She raised up a little and made a face at him, then settled down as if that was her answer to marrying a rich old man.

"I have several good horses you can choose from," she said. "What color do you like?"

"Bay."

"I have a wonderful palomino. He can run like the wind and he has a snowy mane and tail."

"Too fancy for a poor man."

"I have a great blue roan."

"That sounds better."

"No, the yellow horse is much better."

"Not for me."

"He could outrun your enemies."

"But everyone would see him and say that's Margarita Estancia's man."

"Perhaps. Then you would come back to me, no?"

He cupped her face in his hands and kissed her hard on the mouth. Then he held her tight to him. "I won't forget you, my love. No, I won't forget you."

"Good. You can stay at my hacienda tonight."

"Your father, what—"

"He is in Santa Fe. Stay at my *casa*. You can't go anywhere in the dark."

"Only if I may leave before first light."

"Oh, you must have a serious job to do." She raised up and fussed with his vest and shirt until she was satisfied that their arrangement suited her.

"What are they paying you?" she asked.

"Two men who have killed innocent men and raped many women are planning to hurt my friends at Benito. I must stop them."

"Oh, I understand."

He hoped she did. He hoped that he was not too late to stop them. Even with all his hurrying he might still be too slow.

"Are you tired of me?" she asked.

"No, I am concerned for my friends." He hugged her.

"Take the yellow horse, he will get you there quicker."

"We will see."

"I know when you put me off."

"How could I do that?" Then he laughed at her pouting.

She struck his chest with her fist. The blow didn't hurt, but she was no weakling rich girl. In anger, she flailed at him with both hands, but he soon captured her hands.

"Behave. We are in the plaza," he said. She sat up. He released her with a grin. She pertly restored the hat on her head, and looked the prim straight-backed lady again. He allowed her to step down first, then followed. A servant took her bags from the driver. Slocum waited for the man to get his saddle and gear out of the boot.

He thanked the servant and she caught Slocum's arm. "Come along," she said quietly. He went with her and gave her coach driver his saddle, and the man put it in the driver's boot. Then, when they were both in the enclosed coach, the driver clicked to the horses and the iron rims rang on the hard-packed gravelly street.

She quickly cuddled in his arms. He watched out the small slit by the curtains as they stopped for someone to open a large heavy compound gate. Then they entered. The large house was lighted as if for a large party.

"Who is here at the house?" he hissed at her.

"No one, silly."

"Why do they have it all lit up?"

"Oh, they knew I was coming and sometimes I bring many guests."

"They're going to be disappointed tonight."

"I'm not," she said haughtily, and then giggled.

The doorman opened the coach and Slocum stepped out. He felt cramped and his back was stiff from the long ride. The elegant two-story home reminded him of a plantation in the South. On a night like this, there would be an orchestra playing in the front parlor and people waltzing in the hallway on the hardwood floors that had been hand-rubbed with hard wax to a satin finish.

"Come. First you must see the horses." She rushed ahead, dragging him.

"But my saddle—"

"Oh, never mind, they will bring it. Ramon," she shouted. "Get out the golden one."

A sleepy boy rushed to obey her and entered a stall, to return with a dancing palomino on a lead.

"He must be worth a fortune," Slocum said.

"He is the wind." She acted so excited, and impulsively hugged him. "Is he not beautiful?"

"Coronado would have traded his claims for him."

"He was so vain I think he might have. But he is yours."

Slocum shook his head. "You don't understand. I've ridden

some horses to death recently, not through any fault of mine, but I had to get someplace."

"Take him. He is my gift."

"Tell Ramon to put my saddle on him in the morning before the doves call." He was beyond arguing with her.

"You hear him, Ramon?"

The boy nodded and smiled at her. *"Sí, Señorita."*

"Have them bring his saddle from the coach."

"Ah, *sí.*"

Then she gripped Slocum's arm and guided him toward the house. "I have some clothes for you to wear and they will wash yours."

"I smell too much like a horse?"

"Yes, but I love them too."

Slocum closed his eyes, wishing he had more time to savor the luxury she poured upon him. Before the sun came up, he must be on the road to Benito. Damn, his life resembled a dust devil picked up and rolling across the landscape.

Just before down there was a high desert chill. Shaved, bathed, and in his fresh clothes, Slocum checked the cinch. She hugged her arms against the great robe that swallowed her. The yellow horse bounced around, anxious and ready.

"I will see you in few days or . . ." He shrugged.

"You will come back and see me," she said sternly, and with some effort pushed open the large wooden gate into the alley. "Go before I cry for the loss of both of you."

He checked the horse, but the stallion scooted out the gate sideways. Then his iron shoes rang on the hard ground as he pranced on his hind feet the length of the alleyway. In the street and clear of any vehicles or traffic, Slocum let the horse run.

When the wind was in his face, Slocum knew what she'd meant. The horse came from the blood of the king's stables. They raced through the many small farm plots and then up on the tabletop. The animal hardly breathed; Slocum wondered how far the great horse could go at this speed. He had heard of Arabian horses that ran twenty miles without being winded. This fleet animal came from such breeding. In his time he had seen purebred Arabians, but they were smaller than this horse. Few animals he had ever known could match this animal's speed or constitution.

At last he brought the horse down to a swinging walk. He reached Benito at midday, and he undid the leather tie on his Colt's hammer. First he planned to check at the cantina.

"Oh, *mucho caballo*," one man exclaimed, and moved about to inspect Yellow when Slocum dismounted to hitch him at the rack. Soon others did the same, and children came, pointed, and exclaimed. Slocum went inside. He knew the animal would draw way too much attention for him to stay very long.

"You haven't seen Yarborough around here?" he asked the barkeep.

"Not since we drove him away."

"Well, he's coming back. Tell everyone to be ready."

"Oh, *sí, Señor*. This time we will kill him."

"Tell everyone to be ready."

Outside, he had to get the onlookers back. He was afraid the cream-colored horse might step on them in his excitement. He gathered the reins and swung up. Then he checked the horse. With care, he guided him through the crowd and set out up the road for Marcia's. The horse caught people's eyes, and many whistled at him. They looked up from their gardening and farming chores when he passed by.

"What are you riding?" Marcia asked, rushing out of her *casa* to open the gate.

"A great horse I borrowed from the Estancia family in Taos to get here."

"He is beautiful."

"Yes, but Yarborough and Mica are coming back."

"Oh, no."

"I thought they might beat me here."

"No, they are not here. Which way will they come from?"

"The west."

"Then they'll have to cross Polonski's Bridge."

"Yes, they will."

"I will get some things. We can watch out for them there."

"Great idea."

"Will we need others to help us?" she asked, hurrying about to gather things.

"Yes, but I don't know for how long."

"No matter. The men will take their turns. They have vowed never to let anyone do what those men did in this valley ever again."

Slocum pressed his stiff back muscles against the hand-hewn door facing. At least the outlaws weren't there yet. In relief, he closed his eyes. Maybe he would be able to stop them. He hoped so.

25

The small hovel the hermit Polonski had lived in while he constructed the swinging bridge sat tucked under the towering pipes of rock wall that formed the deep canyon. It had long been abandoned, and they found several packrat and bird nests inside it. Marcia busied herself cleaning the place for them to stay in, while Slocum hobbled the palomino horse in a grassy patch under some cottonwoods on the shelf above the river.

Slocum studied the far side of the river and the torturous trail from the top to that side of the bridge. He also counted on the yellow horse to whinny at the approach of any others. A stud horse was not the best riding animal, but in this case, he might make a good watchdog.

"No one has lived here in ages," she said, dumping an armload of sticks and debris outside the front door.

"Beats the stars for a roof, though."

"Oh, yes." She smiled at him and went back to her cleaning.

He gathered up an armload and tossed it aside. Then, seeing she had the bed frame ready, he brought in his gear and the bedroll. As he was busy spreading his ground cloth and blankets over the frame, he turned and listened. A different noise sounded over the rush of the river.

"What is it?" she asked.

"Not certain," he said, and went outside.

A pack train came off the far rim. Slocum went back for his telescope from the saddlebags. In the small eyepiece, he could make out the lead rider, and he didn't look familiar. There was a line of loaded mules behind him. They looked heavily packed. Slocum waited until the tail-end riders came in view, and not recognizing them either, he put up the scope.

"Not them?" she asked quietly.

"No. Someone with a pack train of mules."

"How long before Yarborough gets here?" she asked.

Slocum shrugged. "No idea. I only hope they don't know we're watching the bridge."

"Juan will be here by evening to help you guard it. Other men from the village will take his place."

"I hope it isn't a long time. I was afraid Yarborough might get here before I could. I better go down and ask these men if they've seen him."

"Fine. Now I have the worst shoved outside, I will make you some coffee." She arranged the blouse and reset the waist of her skirt. "I appreciate you coming back for my people's sake."

"No problem. I have a score to settle too. Be back for that coffee." He ambled down the path under the rustling trees to speak to the men after they crossed. Perhaps they had seen some sign of Yarborough. The bray of the jackasses carried across the canyon. They clattered down the rocky trail, and soon filed onto the suspension bridge following a roan bell mare. The sound of their hooves on the planks rang out. He stood back and watched them. Mules would go right into hell behind the butt of a mare.

"Afternoon," the lead man said, coming off the structure. He was a lanky rider with a full beard and a curved back that allowed him to lean forward over the horn when he reined his pony aside.

"Afternoon. Good-looking mules." Slocum could see the operation was businesslike. The man cradled a Winchester and rode a stout-built mountain horse.

"Yeah, good enough." He looked back at the mules as they came off the bridge. "I'm headed for Santa Fe with them."

"Take the tracks on top south, you can't miss it. Say, you didn't see two fellas back there, did you? White men. One is a big man and the other kind of fancy."

"No." He shook his head. "You looking for them?"

"Yes. They're killers. I'd like to head them off."

"Sorry, no help. But good luck. I better get up on top. We come down out of Colorado and ain't seen much more than some coyotes."

Slocum thanked the man and studied the passage of the train. He glanced to the west ridge. Yarborough would be coming. He had to be patient and wait. After the last floppy-eared mule came off the bridge, the tail-end riders, two breeds, nodded to him and rode on.

Slocum went back inside and savored a cup of her coffee.

"What were they packing?" she asked, busy making flour tortillas.

"Never asked."

"What would men find up there to take out?"

"Might be rich ore."

She nodded and went back to her work. He sipped at his coffee.

At midday, he heard braying, and went outside to watch. The local woodcutters had returned from the west. The first of their string dropped off the far rim.

"That is Pedro and Poco. They are brothers," she said, standing beside him outside the doorway.

"They're the ones that Yarborough scattered that day when I came up here."

"Yes. They are good men. I will fix some food and feed them."

"I'll buy some cooking wood from them."

"Good, we may need it." Then she disappeared inside.

Slocum dropped to his haunches. He never enjoyed sitting still for long. This waiting game might try his short patience. He usually took the initiative. But he wouldn't know where to look for the outlaws in the first place, and anyway, if they came back to Benito, this was the most likely place they would pass through.

"Ah, Señor," the small man said, leaning on his staff and regaining his breath. "You are the new bridge keeper?"

"No. I am waiting for some bad men."

"The ones who kidnaped the girls?" His brown eyes widened in shock,

"Yes. Word is they're coming back here."

"Oh." The man shook his sombrero-covered head. "I hope you kill them slowly. They had no respect for anything or anyone."

"I saw them that day when they ran through your train."

"Yes, and worse. But they raped innocent girls. My niece was one."

"Pedro, where is Poco?" she asked, coming outside. "I have some food for both of you."

"Ah, Señora Onza, you would spoil us." He removed his sombrero and looked pleased with her offer.

"I'll go tell his partner," Slocum said, and headed for the bridge. "Oh, yes, she needs some wood. I will buy it."

"Oh, *sí*. We always have good dry wood for her."

"Wash your hands," she said to the man, and pointed to a pan.

Slocum walked to where the loaded burros had collected, and when the other woodcutter rode off the bridge, he greeted him.

"Good afternoon, you must be Poco?" he asked the smaller man on the black burro.

"*Sí*. How are you, Señor?"

"Fine. Señora Onza is up at the hut and she wants to feed you. She also needs some cooking wood."

"I will bring some," he said, and rode his burro into the herd of packed animals. In a minute, he returned leading a loaded one, using his heels to drum his own mount along.

"Ah, I would never miss one of her meals," he added. "I get tired of eating my own cooking when we are up there cutting wood. What is your business here, Señor?"

"I am watching for Yarborough. He is supposed to be coming back."

Poco made the sign of the cross. "When?"

"I don't know, only that he told some people he was headed back for Benito."

"May God have mercy."

"Sorry to upset you," Slocum said, and made a quick check

of the backtrail while he walked beside the man and his animal. Nothing in sight.

"What will you do if he comes, amigo?"

"Kill him."

"Oh, Señor, he is a wicked man."

"That's why."

Nightfall came early in the canyon's depth. Bats fluttered after
insects. Juan arrived and took the first watch armed with Slocum's Winchester. In the small shack, Slocum stretched his
frame out on the top of the bedroll. The day's heat had made
the canyon an oven; now the heat began to dissipate. He was
grateful for the gentle breeze flowing through the room. Before
morning, they would need blankets,

"Wake me when it's my turn to stand guard," he said to
Marcia.

"You were up all day."

"I can still relieve him."

He shut his eyes. The yellow stallion gave a great challenge
that echoed up and down the river. Then there were only the
sounds of the night insects and the river's rush; he fell asleep.

"Slocum. Slocum, wake up," she hissed in his ear.

"What?" he asked softly.

"Juan thinks someone is on the bridge. There is not much
starlight to see by."

"Good. Tell him to stay put." He threw his legs over the
side of the bed frame and quickly pulled on his boots. Had
Yarborough snuck down there? Had the outlaw discovered he
was waiting for him? The man was no fool.

"I told Juan what you said," she said in a low voice when
she returned.

"Did he listen?"

"Yes, I think so. Who do you think is on the bridge?" She
held out his vest to him in the darkness while he strapped on
his holster.

"Probably Yarborough."

"What should we do?"

"Don't let him come off that bridge alive."

"But what do you plan to do?"

"Go out there and meet him. That's why I said don't let him off that bridge alive."

"You worry me. You speak in riddles."

"You will see." He put on his hat and eased out of the dark shack into the inky night. His eyes adjusted, and he could see high above where the rimrock touched the sky, but even the thousands of stars did not shed much light in the depth of the canyon.

She hurried up and caught his arm. "Stay here. Don't go on the bridge by yourself. It is too dangerous."

"No. He needs to be stopped and here is the best place."

"I am worried for you."

"Apaches didn't get me—one or two stinking outlaws won't either." He bent over, lifted her up by her arms, and kissed her on the mouth. When he put her down, she let him go.

He set off in a run for the bridge. When he passed the youth, he gave him a wave. The rush of the river grew louder. In a low crouch, he crossed the last fifty yards to where the thick support ropes were tied off on huge posts planted deep in the ground.

If someone was out there, Slocum couldn't see far enough in the inky night to tell. Glimpses of the cross ropes and the floor supports were all he saw. He felt the main rope on the left side. The vibration of someone or something walking on the structure felt real enough. With care, he eased himself onto the first plank. Step by step, he headed down the swag for the center.

He strained to see whoever was out there. He saw nothing but the black of night and the crisscross of ropes close by that made the bridge work. The slight tilt and twist of the bridge made walking difficult without holding on. Each time he planted a boot heel, he waited until the structure stabilized before taking another step. Then, with his fist closed on the main side rope, he felt the give and take of someone else coming toward him.

Beneath the planks, the river raged in a loud hissing roar. Somewhere ahead was his silent unseen enemy. He thought he saw some movement, and dropped down. The orange muzzle blasts of a revolver spat death into the night.

He aimed his own Colt, but knew the shifting of the bridge and his lack of vision made accurate shooting impossible. Another shot from the gun, and then the hammer clicked on an empty.

"Did you get him?" It was Yarborough calling out. Slocum recognized the voice. So his henchman was on the bridge and Yarborough was backing him up—way back. Slocum heard Mica fight to reload the revolver, and rushed forward. He saw the form and slashed out with his gun barrel. It struck once, drew a groan, and again. Mica sprawled out on the planks.

Slocum stopped, still keenly aware that Yarborough was between him and where the bridge joined the trail on the west. He managed by feel to find the downed man's revolver, and quickly discarded it in the river. Also, a large knife went over. . . .

Half crouched, he waited and listened, hoping that Yarborough would speak again.

"Mica? Mica? Where are you?"

"Throw down your gun," Slocum demanded, and the outlaw answered him with a barrage of bullets that whizzed through the air like angry bees. Then Slocum heard the charge of heavy boots on the planks.

"I'll kill you barehanded!" Yarborough screamed.

Slocum dropped to a crouch to try to see the man's form. But he couldn't, though he twisted his head from side to side. The rage began to gather in his chest. He holstered the Colt, and when satisfied the hurling form coming at him was Yarborough, tackled him around the waist and sprawled him on his back.

His fists found hard flesh, a face, a nose. Yarborough roared like a wounded bear and erupted. He tossed Slocum aside, slamming him into the ropes hard enough to knock the wind out of him. Slocum tried to recover his raging breath. A flying boot struck his leg. He grasped for the man, and took a hard blow to the side of the head. Dazed, he felt Yarborough's powerful hands raise him up. He drove a knee hard into the man's crotch.

His action drew a roar of rage, and he could smell Yarborough's breath in his face. Cool air from the water below swept his face. He drew back and landed a hard blow on the outlaw's cheek. With his back forced against the side ropes, Slocum struggled to stay on the bridge against the herculean force of the man scrambling to push him over.

A world without any light swirled around him, and with the river waiting below, he used every ounce of his strength. Yarborough's fingers bit into his skin. The viselike clamp was so hard and piercing, he knew if he didn't break the man's hold soon he would be forced over the side.

Bad breath, the smells of campfire smoke, horse, and an unwashed human body filled his nostrils. Teeth gritted, he strained to pry the man's hold loose. Inch by inch he lost ground, bent over backwards. He knew as he strained that if something didn't happen soon, he would be tossed in the rushing water of the Rio Grande.

Then Yarborough's foot slipped, he fell to his knees, and the advantage changed. Slocum clouted him with a right and then a left. It spilled the man on the flooring. Yarborough struggled to rise, and then twisted away under Slocum's onslaught and began to run away, barely out of Slocum's grasp.

In full flight, Yarborough half ran, half fell. His swearing and growling filled the night. Slocum was hard on his heels, his breath raging from his aching lungs.

"Come back, you coward!" he rasped.

Hand over hand on the side ropes like a blind man, Slocum climbed the bridge after the man. This worthless raper of innocent girls wasn't getting away this time. The blast of both barrels of a shotgun exploded in the night. In the instant red flash, he saw Yarborough straighten, then spill over backwards from the force of the blast. Slocum could hear the outlaw's body slip down the planks toward him.

"Slocum! Slocum!" Marcia called.

"Here," he said, dropping to his knees.

"Oh, thank God, I thought I had shot you." Marcia clambered over the still body and rushed into his arms.

"You all right?" Juan asked.

"Yes," Slocum said, hugging her. "Get a light. There's another one on the bridge. I stumbled over him back there."

Juan lit a small lamp and held it up. "I knew it was him. I could hear him cussing you."

"You two did good," Slocum told them.

"You are bleeding," she said, concerned.

"I'll be fine—the other—"

"I'll get him. You go with her," Juan said.

In the shack, she lit a candle. With care, she cleansed his cuts and fussed over him. He looked up when Juan entered the room.

"Was he there?"

"*Sí.*"

"You tie him up?"

Juan shook his head. "No. I threw him in the river with Yarborough."

"Oh," Slocum said, and drew a sharp breath. Just as well. Justice had been served.

"You are going to have a bruised face and a black eye," she said, standing with her hands on her hips and appraising him. "Maybe you will heal after a while."

"Maybe," he said, and nodded, pleased. At last it was over.

A week later, with most of the soreness in his body gone, Slocum returned the yellow stallion to Margarita's stables in Taos. No way he could ride such a grand horse without drawing all kinds of unwanted attention. When he learned that the Señorita Estancia was away in Sante Fe, he felt a little sadness at not being able to at least speak to her. However, the stud horse was back where he belonged. The stable keeper who put him up promised to give her his thanks for the use of him.

Slocum mounted the stout strawberry roan in the alleyway. With a salute for the man, he reined the horse around, and headed for Polonski's Bridge. There was lots of country to the west and north he hadn't seen. Time to go take a look at it.